HOPE'S WONDER

A MORGAN'S RUN ROMANCE

M. LEE PRESCOTT

Published by Mt. Hope Press

ISBN: 978-0-9982184-0-3

http://www.mleeprescott.com/

For my beloved family and friends, who fill my life with joy and gratitude.

Chapter 1

Ten miles from Morgan's Run, Hope Seymour wondered if she was making a huge mistake inflicting her misery on Beth Morgan and her family. The hell of the past year dominated her thoughts as she drove, oblivious to the landscape surrounding her. Bruce's death still hurt, and the death of his baby, her baby, haunted her dreams as well as most waking moments. She saw his face, heartbroken when he discovered what she had done, resigned as he scooped her off the floor and drove her to the hospital. "Infection," the physician said as they wheeled her into surgery. Severe infection and hemorrhaging necessitated a hysterectomy to save her life.

Bruce had taken leave and stayed by her side until she recovered, even as she knew it was painful for him to be around her. When her body was healed, he came to her one morning and said, "I'm going back to work. It's undercover below the border so you won't hear from me for a while." A border patrol agent, Bruce spoke fluent Spanish and had taken the dangerous assignment in Mexico that he never would have touched before.

"No, you can't!" she had pleaded. "This is wrong. Please, don't do this!"

He leaned over and kissed her forehead. "It's done, babe."

The pregnancy had been a surprise, the result of a night of sex when they had both been lonely and between partners. She loved Bruce, but she was not in love with him. She knew he felt the same, but also knew that he wanted children more than anything in the world. His strong Catholic faith would never have condoned an abortion.

"I'm sorry," she said, holding on to his arm, eyes pleading.

"Why?" he asked softly, then turned and walked out of her life forever. For the rest of her life, Hope would wonder if her dear friend had accepted the assignment because of her, because his heart and soul had died along with his child. Two months later they found his body in the desert. He had been tortured for days before his death.

Now she was headed to nanny for her friend Beth's baby, due any day. "Are you crazy?" her mother had said when she announced her intention to spend four or five months in Saguaro Valley. "Don't get me wrong, it's beautiful up there, sweetie, but are you ready to be around a baby?"

"I'm fine," Hope had responded. It was a lie, but she knew that being with friends would be healing. Beth and she had met in college and, for a time, had been members of a hiking group organized by Beth's former boyfriend, Bill Sampson. Hope occasionally ran into Bill, but she had dropped out of the group when she moved back to Tintown, a suburb of Tucson.

Hope liked Beth. Her friend was level-headed and kind, qualities Hope very much appreciated. Beth had visited her several times after the abortion, then again when Bruce died. Her presence had been a precious gift. When the offer to nanny arose during one of their weekly phone conversations, Hope had surprised herself and Beth by saying, "Yes!" So, here she was, a few miles from Morgan's Run with no clue if she had made a wise decision or if her mom was right—she really was crazy.

On her few visits to the ranch, she had fallen in love with the loving, raucous Morgan family: parents, two daughters and four sons. Her memories of Morgan's Run were all happy ones—dancing with Beth's brother Robbie at her friend's wedding, riding in the foothills and valley meadows, and hours talking by the fire. Beth's dad was the father she'd always wanted. Her own father, Tom Seymour, had abandoned his young family when Hope was a baby. By all accounts, he was a bastard to his wife and sons. Her mom was now on her third husband, Ralph, and had finally found a nice guy, stable, loving, and financially secure. *Will I ever find that?* Hope wondered as she turned off the Gila Highway.

Chapter 2

"Great to have you home, buddy," Ben Morgan said, reaching over to pat his younger brother's shoulder.

"Great to be home," Robbie said. "Does Spark need any help for the big wedding, do you think?" He referred to Spark Foster, his father's college roommate, who had recently moved from Portland, Oregon, built an enormous home and was now preparing to host his daughter, Amy's wedding to Jeb Barnes, a wrangler at the ranch.

"Not that we've been told. According to Dad, he has a small army over there."

Robbie laughed. "Yeah, billionaires can do that, can't they- hire armies to do their bidding?" Spark Foster had made his fortune in solar and wind power, and his company, Portland Alternative Power, now run by his hand-picked successors, was the largest of its kind on the west coast.

The brothers sat with their sisters, Beth and Ruthie, in Beth's spacious, sunny kitchen, glorious views of the western Valley in front of them.

Beth's first baby was four days overdue. She gave Robbie a tired smile, patting his hand. "Never mind Spark. We need all the help we can get around here."

"Dad said you might need an extra hand at the farm."

"Things are slower right now and the men are doin' a terrific job."

"And what about me?" Ruthie asked, chin jutted out, hands on hips.

Beth laughed. "Sorry, I meant to say, Ruthie and the guys. I can manage my part from the house for a few months now that Lang's finished my office."

"Almost finished,'" her husband said, stepping into the kitchen, hammer in hand. "Hey, Robbie, didn't hear you come in." Beth's tall, lanky husband brushed sandy hair from his face as he came forward to shake his brother-in-law's hand.

"Hey, Lang, lookin' good," Robbie said, green eyes gazing up. "Can I help in there?"

"Almost done. Just a couple of trim pieces then we can move my bride into her sanctuary." He bent, kissing the top of Beth's head. "How long you in town?"

"Couple of weeks." Robbie watched the interplay between Lang and his sister, wondering if he'd ever find anyone who made him feel like that. Their love was palpable. "Dad's pressuring me to relocate, as you know, but maybe in a year or two. He looks good, by the way. Has he been healthy?"

"Pretty good. You'd never know his heart is failing. We're always praying the doctors are wrong," Beth said as she looked up at Robbie.

Unlike her other brothers, Robbie had green eyes and sandy hair. This Morgan son favored their mother, Leonora. He had departed the Valley for college and rarely returned for long. After graduating from University of Colorado, he had stayed in Boulder, working for a few years before moving to Sedona, where he was co-manager of a very successful outdoor adventure tours company. Ben Morgan Senior had been begging him to come home to run a similar touring company on the ranch. Robbie's answer was always, "No red clay here, Dad." He knew the kinds of tours he and his partners ran would be highly successful here in the valley of his birth, but he hated to share Saguaro with hoards of outsiders. Also, while he loved his family more than life itself, he also valued his independence.

"If Dad and Mom had their way, we'd all be living on the ranch, or close by," Beth said.

"Not Sam," Ruthie said, referring to the second Morgan brother, who had recently moved to Maryland with Lang's sister, Rose.

"No, not Sam, but I wouldn't be surprised if they come back someday," Ben said.

"When am I gonna see my niece and nephew?" Robbie asked him. "Where are they, anyway? And where is my beautiful sister-in-law?"

"Maggie and the kids went to Ned's for breakfast," Ben said, referring to his father-in-law, Ned Williams, who lived in town. "You'll see 'em soon enough, at dinner tonight."

"Can't wait."

The front door bell sounded. "Oh, that must be Hope. Will you go, sweetheart?" Beth asked, gazing up at her husband.

As Lang disappeared, Robbie gazed from brother to sister. "Hope?"

"Beth's friend from Tucson," Ruthie said. "You remember, the woman you were all over at their wedding."

"Was not!" Robbie said, recalling Beth's lovely colleague from U of A.

"Another example of the Morgan boys lovin' em and leavin' em," Ruthie said, flipping her red ponytail.

"Hush, Ruthie," Beth said as she turned to Robbie. "She's coming to stay for a few months to help with the baby."

He was about to ask how she could get time off from work when Lang and Hope came into the kitchen. With Ben's assistance, Beth rose, opening her arms to hug her friend.

"So good to see you, Hope! Did Lang get your bags?"

"They're in the truck. We'll get 'em later. Look at you!" she said, stepping back.

"Yes, I'm the size of a hippo."

"You look gorgeous," Hope said, smiling at her friend.

And so do you, Robbie thought, watching the two women. Hope was dressed in jeans and a plaid shirt, sleeves rolled to her elbows and collar open. The shirt's azure background was reflected in her arresting blue eyes. Her blond hair, in one long braid, trailed down her back, almost to her waist. He noticed stains on her shirt sleeves and remembered Hope was a painter, a good one. Beth and Lang had several of her paintings hanging in their home, including a large landscape of the Valley on their kitchen wall. *Was she that pretty last year?*

"You remember my family," Beth said, stepping back, waving round the room.

"Yes, hello everyone," Hope said.

Is it my imagination, or did she blanch when she spied me? Robbie thought. *Oh, cripes, what kind of shit was I at that wedding?*

Hope's gaze darted from Robbie to his siblings. She daren't gaze too long at those green eyes or they would suck her in all over again. If she didn't watch out, Robbie Morgan and his killer smile would have her swooning. She remembered the feel of his strong arms as he held her, sweeping her round the dance floor on that magical evening. Warning bells sounded and she shook herself. *Never again. You're here to heal, not fall in love again. Besides, after the past six months, I want nothing to do with men, especially Robbie Morgan!*

Beth gazed from her sandy-haired brother to her friend, their attraction electric. Sensing Hope's unease, she said, "Well, I'm up now. Let's get you settled in."

"There'll be no settling-in assistance from you, my beautiful, headstrong mother-to-be," Lang said.

Beth rolled her eyes. "I can supervise."

"Whatever you say, sweetie. Come on, guys. Take five minutes."

The group followed Hope to her truck, a battered, dusty blue Tacoma. The back held a number of boxes and several suitcases as well as an easel. Ben Morgan eyed the lot and asked, "You movin' in permanently?"

Hope laughed. "No, but I had to bring my painting gear. I've got a major show in April and will need to work in the evenings and at nap time."

Ben grinned. "Nap time, you wish."

Beth swatted him. "Hope will not be on duty 24-7. We parents will be with baby Dillon most of the time, thank you very much. I'm cutting my hours at the farm and working from home, and Lang's schedule is really flexible. We are so grateful for Hope's help, but this is also meant to be a sabbatical or getaway for her."

Robbie watched Hope's face drain of color and wondered what had really brought her to the Valley for such an extended period. He turned to his sister. "Where are we takin' this stuff, boss?"

"Rooms to the left at the top of the stairs. She's using the first as her studio. It has the best light."

Robbie grabbed a large box. As he lifted it out of the truck bed, Hope came to his side and his elbow brushed against her left breast, its softness sending shock waves through him. *Whoa, boy!* he thought as she jumped back.

Hope shivered right down to her toes and her knees wobbled. *This is not going to happen!*

CHAPTER 3

The group made short work of Hope's unloading. When all the boxes and bags had been deposited in her two rooms at the top of the stairs, she took a deep breath, hands on hips. "That's it, guys. Thank you. Just leave everything and I'll unpack later."

As everyone congregated in the kitchen once again, Ben said, "Okay, guys and gals, I'm outta here. Gotta meet Maggie and the kids."

"Wait," Ruthie cried, barring the door to the living room. "I thought Maggie was coming here?"

"Nope. Now move aside, Shortcake. I'm already late."

Ruthie stayed put, chin out, as she stared at her big brother, then scanned the room, all eyes on her, wondering at her strange behavior.

"I'm engaged."

"Ha, ha, outta the way, Shortcake," Ben said, patting her shoulder.

Ruthie stood her ground. "I'm serious. I'm engaged."

Robbie raised his hands. "To who?"

"Kevin, of course," she said, referring to Kevin Statler, a man she'd been dating for the past month.

"Another Internet guy?" Robbie asked, gazing from his sister to their older siblings.

Beth shook her head and Ben shrugged.

"When the hell did this happen?" Ben asked, chestnut eyes serious now. "Did you know about this, Bethie?"

"No, she didn't. He proposed last night and I said yes. I wanted to tell you all together before we tell Mom and Dad."

"Which you are never going to do."

"Stop it, Ben," Beth said. "Let's all sit down and hear her out."

"There's nothing to hear. I'm engaged. I'm gonna tell the folks tonight, period. I'm just sorry Maggie's not here. She'd be happy for me."

"We are!" Beth moved forward to hug her youngest sibling and business partner, glaring over Ruthie's shoulder at her brothers. "It's just a bit of a shock, sweetie."

"Shock," Robbie said. "That's an understatement, don'cha think?"

"Where is Statler, anyway?" Ben asked. "I'd like to have a word with him."

"You'll see him tonight and you're not going to say anything. I mean it, Ben!"

"Shortcake, this is crazy. We have to—"

"Don't call me that!"

"You can't just up and marry someone you just met," Robbie said, coming to stand beside their older brother and sister.

"I didn't just meet him. We've been dating for –"

"About a minute," Ben said, eyes blazing now.

"Does Harley know?" Beth asked softly.

Ruthie's cheeks turned bright red. "Of course not! We just decided last night. Besides, it's none of his business!"

"He loves you, Ruthie, and you love him," Beth said.

"Too bad. He had his chance and he blew it. I love Kevin now."

"Why don't we believe you?" Robbie asked, eying his sister.

"This is bullshit," their oldest brother said. "And I forbid you to tell Mom and Dad. He'll have a heart attack."

"No he won't. He likes Kev."

"Yeah, as in 'Welcome to the ranch, dude,' not 'Hey, son, glad you're joining the family.'"

Ruthie broke away from her siblings and approached Lang. "I suppose you feel the same way?"

"Hey, don't look at me. This seems like a Morgan family matter."

"News flash—when you married Beth you became part of this family. So you approve?"

"Hard to say. Have only met the man once or twice. Seems nice enough, but why the hurry?"

"We love each other and we're getting married. We're only telling the family now so we don't steal Amy and Jeb's thunder. We'll make a big announcement after the wedding."

Ben shook his head. "I repeat, this is bullshit. I'm goin' to get Mag and the kids. Then you and I are getting into this, sis."

"Are not!" Ruthie turned and stalked out of the kitchen. "And thank you all for your well wishes on my special day. They mean so much!"

"Come back here, Ruthie!" Ben said.

Beth grabbed his arm. "Let her go."

"This is craziness."

"Of course it's craziness," Beth said, "but if you yell and scream at her, she's just going to dig in her heels."

"You sure you didn't know about this?"

She shook her head. "Not a peep. They do talk quite often. I've caught her sitting in the office on the phone a lot."

"I'll talk to her," Robbie said. "I've gotta head out, too. Hope, good to see you again." His eyes lingered on Beth and Lang's soon-to-be nanny, all but forgotten during the melee over Ruthie's announcement.

Hope nodded. "Yes, see you soon, I expect."

Beth observed the interplay between her brother and her friend. "Very soon. We're all coming to dinner tonight. We wouldn't want to miss the fireworks."

"Jesus Christ," Ben muttered, shoving Robbie through the door in front of him.

Beth gave her a weary smile. "Welcome to Morgan's Run. Never a dull moment around here."

CHAPTER 4

"Your brothers are still gorgeous, I see," Hope said as she and Beth walked arm in arm in the shade of the back terrace.

"Hmm, all I see is the hellions who drove me crazy as kids," Beth said, settling onto a two-person swing and patting the seat beside her.

Hope sat, rubbing her friend's shoulder. "Bet they're there for you in a crisis."

"Always."

"You're so lucky."

"How're you doing, dearie?"

"It's good to get away. My mom swoops in and out offering all kinds of advice, and everyone who comes into the shop wants to offer their condolences."

"Of course they do. That's a close-knit neighborhood."

"Especially when you're born and raised there. Only time I got away was our four years at U of A."

"Seems like forever, doesn't it?" Beth patted her belly, then instantly regretted it. Hope had insisted she was ready to nanny their baby, but Beth wondered if it might be too soon, too much for her, especially on top of Bruce's death.

Bruce Cobb and Hope Seymour had been friends since childhood and on-and-off lovers as adults. Hope always said the lovers part was a mistake, but they often found themselves in one another's arms when other relationships broke up. They were not together when Hope discovered she was pregnant, but the child was his.

Beth also knew that Hope had gone for the abortion without telling him and that the friends were estranged when he died. How terribly tragic it was.

Sensing her friend's discomfort, Hope reached over and squeezed her hand. "It's okay, Bethie. I'm really happy for you and Lang and can't wait to help with the baby. I promise you won't find me weeping or sneaking off in the night with your child."

"But you'll tell me if it's too much?"

"Absolutely, but that goes for you, too. I am so incredibly grateful to be here, but if having me around drives you crazy, you need to give me the boot."

"Never! We're thrilled. Why did we build this big ole house if not to fill it with friends and loved ones?"

Hope smiled, then turned to gaze across the valley. "This terrace reminds me of your folks' backyard."

"We all have them. You haven't seen Ben and Maggie's place, have you? When we built, both my brother and I replicated our favorite place at the big house."

"What an incredible view."

"Yes," Beth sighed, leaning back.

"You are so lucky."

"Yes, we are."

Hope reached over and took her hand. "Thanks for being here to meet me."

"My pleasure. What would you like to do?"

"Settle in, if that's okay?"

"Perfect. Will give me time to putter in the nursery."

"So happy for you, Beth. Baby boy or girl Dillon is gonna be one lucky kiddo."

*****

Did I make a mistake? Hope mused as she stowed the last of her clothes in the wardrobe. Between grieving Bruce's death and the abortion and subsequent hysterectomy, it had been a terrible time. She might be physically healed, but in every other way she was a red-hot mess. *Maybe not the best time for Robbie Morgan to come back into my life.* Still, she felt at peace in Beth and Lang's home and so grateful for the chance to get out of Dodge. She loved Tintown, but everyone knew everyone and right now, there was no peace for her in the shop or at home. Her partner, Alice Wilkes, was happy to mind the shop, an artist's co-op where Hope sold her work and that of many others.

"Go, sweetie. Get out while you can!" Alice had told her. Her partner also found a tenant for Hope's cottage behind the shop, which was an enormous relief.

"Thank you, Alice," Hope said aloud, gazing around at her beautiful bedroom. *Nantucket,* she thought, unless one looked out the large west-facing windows at the green valley and mountains beyond. The four-poster queen bed and matching end tables and dresser were pine, a chunky cottage style, painted in distressed off-white. The patchwork quilt in pale shades of blue and green went perfectly with a deep, comfortable chair upholstered in fabric that swirled with faded blue hyacinths and greenery. The bathroom echoed the beachy theme with bowls of seashells and soft sea foam walls. "Lang loves Nantucket and Cape Cod," Beth had told her when they were building. "So we have the best of both worlds. The southwest downstairs and seashore upstairs."

Someone with incredible taste had decorated this room. While she knew her friends were talented, Hope suspected that Leonora Morgan, Beth's mother, had had a hand here. Lang's mom, Martha, was no slouch in the decorating department, either.

As she headed into the adjacent room to set up her studio, Hope smiled at her reflection in a mirror framed in sea glass and shells. *You can be happy here, even if it's only for a short while.*

CHAPTER 5

Robbie declined Ben's invitation to drive into town and headed to the big house instead. Over his mother's strong objections, he had promised his father he'd go for a short ride with him. When he arrived, he found Leonora Morgan in the kitchen chatting with Carmela, their cook and housekeeper.

Leonora smiled, brushing a lock of blond hair from her forehead, leaving a trace of what looked like flour behind. "Hey, sweetie, come join us. Want some iced tea or a sandwich?"

"That'd be great. Where's Dad?"

"Napping, which is where he should stay! You know I don't like him riding." Hands on hips, she glared at her fourth-born. Her thick blond hair was tied back in a scarf, and she wore jeans and a green beaded top, a crisp white apron tied round her tiny waist. His parents turned sixty in a few months, but one would never know gazing at Leonora Morgan. She was still a beauty.

"We're only doin' the ranch loop and maybe a short detour to climb Pete's Ridge."

"I'm sure your father'll be champing at the bit to go further."

"It's the horse that champs."

"Ha, ha!"

Carmela watched the two, a bemused look on her face. "What can I get you, Mr. Robbie?"

Carmela had been with the family since her teens. She and her husband, Raoul, lived in one of the ranch cottages. He managed the farm's livestock, working alongside Robbie's sister's Beth, who ran the office and processing barns, and Ruthie, who oversaw the gardens. Despite his mother's tendency to snobbery, she and her plump, dark-skinned housekeeper were dear friends and constant companions. It was a mystery to her offspring how Carmela, whom they all adored, had put up with their mother all these years. Childless, the housekeeper treated the Morgan children as her own and had always been a loving, indulgent third parent.

"Robbie, please, Carm," he said, going through the same ritual they did every time he visited. Even after all these years, she refused to drop the formality. "If you have bacon, I'd love a BLT, but anything's fine."

"Avocado, too?"

"Please." He smiled at her. "You know, Carm, I dream of your food in Sedona."

"There's a simple answer to that," his mother said. "Move back home where you belong."

"No can do right now. Maybe someday."

"Your father needs you."

"Yer ole dad's hangin' on just fine, thank you. Ain't dead yet." Ben Morgan Senior, all six feet six of him, swung open the door from the dining room, blue eyes twinkling, huge grin on his handsome craggy face. Never so happy than when his children were in residence, he'd been whistling all week at the prospect of the entire clan home from Christmas through New year's.

"Hey, Pop. You had lunch yet?"

"Nope. Carmela, honey, fix me whatever yer fixin' my buddy here."

"BLT with avocado?"

"Perfect." He perched on a stool, one elbow resting on the huge island crafted with birch from the ranch's north woods. "So, what's new at yer sister's? She okay?"

"Ready to pop, but doin' fine."

Leonora threw up her hands. "This wait is killing us!"

Ben Senior grabbed his wife round the waist, drawing her to him for a hug and kiss. "Now, Mama, baby'll come in his or her own sweet time."

"Oh, pish tush," she said, turning to Robbie. "Was Ruthie with you? She knows I need her this afternoon. She promised to help Carm and me with tonight's dinner."

"She was there, but don't know what's she's up to now."

"No good, I'm sure. That girl's gonna be the death of me. She insists on bringing that dull Keith to our family dinner tonight!"

"Aren't you havin' the whole crew—Dillons, Fosters and Harley and the guys?"

"Yes, but they're family! We hardly know Keith, for goodness' sake!"

Ben Senior nuzzled her neck. "It's Kevin, darling, and he's a nice fella."

"Dull as dishwater. Besides, it's very awkward with Harley and Willow coming. Leave it to your sister," she said, rolling her eyes at Robbie as she wriggled out of her husband's grasp.

Carmela set down the sandwiches and tall glasses of iced tea, a bowl of chips beside them.

Robbie smiled at her. "Thanks, Carm."

"So, has that pretty nanny arrived?" his father asked, taking a sip of tea.

Robbie choked on his first bite of sandwich, nodding.

Eyes narrowed, Leonora stared at him. "You okay, honey?"

Ben Senior winked at her. Neither parent had missed his shameless flirting with Beth's Tucson friend at the wedding. "How's she doin'?" he asked, blue eyes studying his blond-haired boy, Nora's boy.

"Fine, I guess."

Never one to shy away from an inquisition, his mother said, "Your dad and I thought you might be sweet on her when she came for Beth's wedding. She's a major Southwest painter, you know."

"No, I didn't," he said, realizing he knew next to nothing about Hope Seymour. "The painting at Beth and Lang's are pretty cool."

Leonora waved her hand. "She shows at all the major galleries here. In fact, I've heard that her work is now in Boston, New York, and Chicago as well as up and down the West Coast."

"Impressive," he said, but his mind was on other things. Those sky-blue eyes, a body that her torn jeans and frayed flannel shirt couldn't quite hide, the remembrance of her full, soft breasts pressed against him as they danced.

His mother gave him sharp look. "Robert, your father asked you a question."

"Sorry, Dad. Daydreaming, I guess."

About a blond-haired bohemian, Ben Senior mused, smiling at his son. *Perfect match, if I've ever seen one. Too bad he's as pig-headed as the rest of 'em.* "No problem. I was just talking about Ms. Seymour. Your sister says she's had a pretty rough year."

"In what way?" Robbie asked, polishing off the last bite of his sandwich.

"Beth says she lost a dear friend," Leonora said. "That's all she's said, but I'll wager there's a lot more to that story."

"Now, Nora," her husband said, patting her hand. "Not our business."

"It certainly is our business. If the woman's going to be caring for our grandchild, we need to know that she's stable."

"Seemed pretty stable to me," Robbie said, shooting a conspiratorial look at his father.

"Are Ms. Beth and Mr. Lang ready for the baby?" Carmela asked, setting a plate of freshly baked cookies on the table.

"Ready as anyone ever is, I guess," Robbie said. "Baby's room looks great and Lang was finishing work on Beth's office today. He's an amazing finish carpenter. Have you seen the built-ins he's put in?"

"Not this week," his mother replied, eyes lost in thought. "I think Carmela and I should head up there tomorrow, see if there's any last-minute work to be done."

"You two have already stocked their freezer with enough food to last a decade," her husband said.

"Ha, ha. Aren't you two going somewhere?"

Ben Senior rose, kissed his wife's cheek and patted Robbie's shoulder. "I'm ready when you are, partner."

Chapter 6

Ben Morgan sat in the shadow of the barn, two-year-old son, Ben the third, on his lap. They were watching Emma, his seven-year-old, feed apples to Jadie, her Aunt Ruthie's pinto. Her mother, Maggie, stood nearby talking to her assistants, Jeb Barnes and Nick Parker. Ben still couldn't believe how these two women and now baby Ben had turned his life upside down.

Three years ago, he'd been leading a 24-7 California bachelor life. After a cardiac episode, he had returned home to rest, unaware that a daughter, *his daughter*, and her brave, amazing mother waited in his beloved Valley. Emma had been conceived during a memorable one-night stand with wrangler Maggie Williams just before he hightailed it out of town to start a West Coast business with two of his college friends. Now married to the love of his life, he oversaw ranch operations for his parents and did whatever was needed, including leading pack trips with his best friend, Harley Langdon, who ran the stables. Ben and Maggie also ran Emma's Dream, a summer camp for handicapped children that had been in operation for two summers.

"That's enough apples, Sweet Pea," he called as Emma pulled the fifth from the bag.

"Uncle Robbie! Grandpa!" she cried, spying father and son coming out of the barn with Royal and Thor. Royal was Ben Senior's horse, a steady, beautiful morgan. Thor was a tall, gangly Friesian. Thor had been a rescue and the wranglers, especially Nick Parker, had worked for months to rehabilitate the proud horse from an abusive owner. Now his black coat shone and he stepped briskly, shaking his head as Robbie tied him to the fence.

Emma leaped into her grandfather's arms as her uncle tousled her chocolate curls. "Hey, Peanut. How's my favorite niece?"

"Great. What're ya doing? Are you and Grandpa goin' riding?"

"Yup."

"Can I come, please, can I, can I, *please*?" Her eyes darted from her adoring grandfather to Robbie, then her parents.

Maggie shook her head. "Not on Jadie."

"Can I ride the Loop with Uncle Robbie to get Sunny?" she asked, referring to her pony.

"Absolutely not!" her mother said. It had been less than a year since Maggie had fallen on the Loop Trail, causing her to miscarry. That memory as well as a constant fear for Emma's safety were never far from her mind.

"Hey, Mags, why don't I drive her to the house real quick? Rob and Dad can meet us there. We'll have Sunny ready to go."

Hands on hips, Maggie regarded her husband. "You haven't even bothered to ask your Dad or Robbie if they're okay with it. Maybe they weren't planning to ride the loop."

"You kiddin'?" her father-in-law said. "My little cowgirl's always welcome."

Robbie smiled at his gorgeous sister-in-law, glimpsing the tears that rimmed her deep blue eyes. He knew only too well the ordeal she'd been through with Emma's accident, paralysis, surgery and rehabilitation. "It's fine with us, Mags, but if you need her here, then—"

"Can I, so can I, can I? Please, Mommy!"

Maggie threw up her hands. "Okay, but you stay close and listen to Grandpa and Uncle Robbie."

"Yes, Mommy!" The child ran to hug her mother.

"I'll take Ben," Maggie said, reaching for the child.

"No, hon, he's fine. You're busy and I have some stuff to do at the house. I'll take my little buddy. After we get Em off, I'll give him an early lunch and put him down for a nap."

"Thanks," she said, rubbing his arm as he bent to kiss her. "You be a good boy for Daddy, sweetie." She kissed the chubby cheeks and smoothed back his damp brown curls.

As Ben and his children disappeared, Robbie and Ben Senior mounted and prepared to head out. Maggie walked over and patted Royal's nose, gazing up at her father-in-law, then Robbie. "Has she spoiled your plans?"

"No way, sweetie," her father-in-law said.

She laughed. "I know that's what you'd say, you old softie. Robbie, is this really okay?"

"Absolutely. We had no plans. I asked Dad to go riding so I could get some practice. We weren't planning to go far."

"Well, then, thank you, and be careful. What trail are you taking off the loop?"

"We thought maybe Pete's Ridge."

"Well, watch the north side. I took a lesson up there a few days ago and there's been some washout after the last storm. Have you got water? It's supposed to be hotter than Hades in a while. Please makes sure Emma drinks lots of water."

Ben Senior smiled down at her. "Will do, and don't worry, darlin'. We'll take good care of her."

"I know you will," she said. "Now git or my daughter'll be heading out to meet you."

CHAPTER 7

As they reached a bend in the trail out of earshot of the stables, Robbie turned to his father. "Maggie's still hurting, isn't she?"

"Been through a lot, that's true. Between Emma's accident, her surgery, and the fall, ya can't blame her for worrying. But our Maggie's a strong woman."

"That's for sure."

When Emma was two, a drunk driver had hit Maggie's car, paralyzing the child. Two years later, when Ben, Emma's dad, came back into their lives, doctors told Ben and Maggie that surgery might help their daughter to walk again. Knowing the risk, they finally agreed to go ahead with the surgery. There followed months of grueling rehab during which the Morgan family and Ned Williams, Maggie's father, had created Team Emma to support the child and her parents. Members of Team Emma had kept a secret until the day of Ben and Maggie's wedding, when their brave daughter had walked down the aisle on her Uncle Robbie's arm.

"So how're you doin', Dad? You been feelin' okay?"

"Right as rain. Now that your brother's pretty much taken over, I'm on easy street. Plenty of time for long naps and a little evening schmoozing at the Lodge."

Robbie laughed. "And, no one does it better than you."

"Nappin' or schmoozing?"

"Both."

"Have more time for your mother. That is when she's not involved in all her activities. Spark's here now, too, and he's always up for an adventure."

"How is Spark?"

"Never better. Haven't seen him much with Amy and Jeb's wedding planning. He calls when he wants to get out of the line of fire. Your mother is helping."

"So I heard. How's the house coming along?"

"Completed. He moved in after Thanksgiving. It's a showplace. Barn, too. Wait'll you see it. Spared no expense. Sam did a terrific job."

His brother Sam, an architect, once based in Flagstaff, was now living and working in Maryland with his fiancée, Rose Dillon. Before their departure, he had designed and overseen the construction of his billionaire client's dream house. *Showplace* was an understatement.

"Sam's a genius. We all know that. When do they get here?"

"Christmas Eve."

"Cutting it close, aren't they?"

"Rose has surgery that morning. She didn't want to postpose since they're staying on after the wedding." His brother's fiancée was a pediatric neurosurgeon and daughter of the elder Morgans' dear friends and neighbors, Jay and Martha Dillon.

"When's my little brother get in?" Kyle, the youngest Morgan brother was completing veterinary training in Boston."

"Tonight, Ben's pickin' him up."

"Big house's gonna be full again, huh?"

"Sam and Rose are staying with the Dillons so it'll be just you, Ruthie, and Kyle. Your mother is fearful that Ruthie will want Mr. Statler to stay, but perhaps he'll head home for the holidays."

If they only knew the news coming tonight. "What'd you think of Mr. Statler, Dad?"

"Nice enough kid. Don't see it goin' anywhere unless Harley hightails it."

"Never. He's as much a part of this place as you are."

"Maybe, but he has Willow to think about." Willow was Harley's fifteen-year-old daughter, conceived during his college years, but unknown to him until a year earlier when her mother had contacted him.

"How is Willow's mom?" Robbie asked. Talia Goldstein was dying of aggressive, stage four breast cancer.

"Up and down. She sounds like a fighter. Has tried every treatment in the book."

"Ben said Harley's been helping out there."

"He can afford it."

"Oh?"

"Has deep pockets, our head wrangler. He's a savvy investor and saves every penny. He also inherited some family money, according to your brother. I imagine he's invested that well. Lives in that hole-in-the-wall place in town even though we've offered him one of the ranch cabins many times. Never know what drives a man.

"Hey, son, who's that ahead? Don't know who's under that Stetson, but that's Martha Dillon's Whimsy he's riding."

CHAPTER 8

Robbie followed his father's gaze, recognizing the faded flannel shirt and blond braid draped over her shoulder. "It's not a he, Dad. It's Beth's friend, Hope Seymour."

"Oh?"

"Yup, the new nanny." *And boy, can she ride.*

His father nudged Royal and the horse trotted ahead. "Howdy-do, Ms. Seymour! Welcome back to the Valley." As she drew nearer, the elder Morgan slid off his horse and doffed his hat.

She smiled at the handsome, gray-haired patriarch, a smile that lit up her beautiful face. "Three Morgan men in one day. How's a girl get this lucky?"

"Two more on the way. They're all be here soon, darlin', so you won't know where to look." He reached up to take her hand as she dismounted and gave him a hug.

"So good to see you again, Mr. Morgan."

"Never mind the Mr. Morgan stuff. Ben'll do just fine, as I told you on your last visit."

She laughed. "That could get confusing. There are a few Bens around here." As she spoke, Hope was acutely aware of the other man standing beside his father. It was as if his heat radiated out, enveloping her. *Step back, Hope!* "Hello. We meet again," she said.

"Hey, Hope." Robbie stared at her. *Pull yourself together, man!*

Ben Senior observed his son thoughtfully before turning to her. "You sure know your way around a saddle, darlin'."

"Been riding since I was three. My Uncle Randy has a farm. I helped out summers and after school." She glanced at Robbie out of the corner of her eye as he removed his faded blue baseball cap to wipe his brow. All the Morgan men were handsome, including the gray fox in front of her, but this blond, green-eyed Adonis was exceptional. His broad shoulders strained the fabric of his faded ranch tee shirt. While his dad was long and lean, Robbie at barely six feet was all wiry muscle. She knew he was a guide in Sedona, a job that required strength and agility. *They don't make 'em that way in Tintown,* she mused.

"Where are you cowboys headed?"

"We're picking up my granddaughter, then taking a short ride. Care to join us?"

"Thanks, but I wouldn't want to intrude."

"Nonsense. We'd like the company, wouldn't we, son?"

"You're the boss, Dad." Robbie took a deep breath and gave her a hundred-watt grin. Sure, come along. We won't be out more than an hour or so, and Emma loves to show people her riding prowess."

"I will, then," she said, mounting Whimsy with grace and ease. "It'll be nice to get the lay of the land with you. Thanks so much."

"Our pleasure," Ben Senior said, mounting Royal as Robbie hopped up on Thor again.

They proceeded slowly with Ben Senior in the lead. This left Robbie and Hope riding side by side.

"That's quite a horse you're riding," she said, forcing her attention from his gorgeous body to the tall black stallion. "What is he?"

"A Friesian. The ranch rescued him last summer. He's made an amazing recovery thanks to Ned Williams and Nick Parker."

"Ned's Maggie's dad, isn't he?"

"Best vet in a hundred miles even if he never finished school," Ben said over his shoulder. "And Parker's turned out to be a regular horse whisperer."

"Parker?" she asked. He gazed over, giving her the Morgan smile. *Could charm the pants off a woman,* Hope mused, *but not me. I'm not falling again.*

"Ranch's newest wrangler," he said, wondering at her sudden frown. "Nick works with Harley, Maggie, and Jeb at the stables. They hired him to help with lessons and general chores, which he does, but it turns out that he's amazing with the horses. You know they train wild mustangs for the Border Patrol?"

"Yes, Beth told me something about that. Is your horse headed south?"

"No, not ole Thor. We'll keep him here. When he's a little stronger, he should be fine for pack trips."

"You said 'we' just now. That mean you're planning to settle back here soon?"

He laughed. "No, that was the family 'we.' Maybe someday."

Her blue eyes danced with mischief and her sweet, luscious lips parted in a lovely, slightly crooked smile. *There's something about her,* Robbie thought, watching her adjust herself in the saddle. Women threw themselves at him on almost every tour he led, and Robbie Morgan had had his share of girlfriends in his twenty-nine years, but none as intriguing as Hope Seymour.

"You're lucky with your family, you know," she said quietly.

"Yeah, we are. What about your folks?"

"Mom's in Tucson, on her third husband. Dad left when my brothers and I were little. I don't remember him. According to Mom, he wasn't a very nice guy." His beautiful green eyes looked sad. "It's been okay. Really."

Why don't I believe you? He grinned. "When my dad's not along, we'll have to take a longer ride sometime. You can give me a pointer or two."

She laughed. "I doubt that."

Just ahead, Ben Senior called, "Hey, there's my cowgirl!" as he and Royal headed down the path leading to his son's backyard.

"Hi, Grandpa! I'm ready."

His son on his left arm, Emma's dad held the pony's halter. "Okay, guys, she's champin' at the bit, and I don't mean Sunny." Ben spied Hope and nodded. "Hey, Hope. Glad you're along to keep these guys in line. Take good care of my baby."

"Will do," she called, marveling at the easy charm of the eldest Morgan brother. *Doesn't hurt that he's gorgeous as hell!*

CHAPTER 9

As the four made their way up the trail, Emma chattered away to her grandfather who rode alongside her. Robbie and Hope brought up the rear, each aware of the other's nearness.

"She's a doll, your niece."

"Yup, she's our miracle, alright."

"Beth's told me about her surgery and all."

"Bravest little girl in the world. She went into her surgery like a trooper, then worked her tiny heart out in rehab. Watching her, I'm pretty sure it hurt like hell getting her legs back into action, but she never gave up. She pushed and pushed and pushed so she could walk down the aisle at the wedding."

"Her parents must have been stunned."

"Wasn't a dry eye in the house."

"What a moment."

He turned and gave her a warm smile. "Yeah, Em's pretty special. Got any kids in your family?"

"A niece and nephew, but I don't see them much." Hope turned away, but not before he glimpsed tears in her eyes.

Robbie watched as she nudged Whimsy forward. *What is that about?* Baffled, he followed. All of a sudden, Emma's chattering stopped and she cried out, "What's the matter, Grandpa?"

Royal paused, nickering softly as his rider slumped in the saddle. Robbie jumped to the ground and ran ahead. Hope followed, grabbing hold of Sunny's halter as she neared Emma's side. The child's eyes were wide with terror and she was trembling.

Ben Senior was white as a sheet, eyes closed, as Robbie slid him off the horse. "Dad! What is it? Are you in pain?" He settled him on soft ground at the trail's edge, then grabbed the canteen strapped to Royal's saddle and removed his father's bandana, soaking it with water and dabbing it on his face.

At once, his father opened his eyes and gave him a wan smile. "Hey, don't drown me, son. I'm okay. Just this heat. Help me up, now, will you?"

"Nothing doing. Hope, can you take Emma back to Ben's? They have a golf cart. Have 'em bring it, will you?"

"You'll do no such thing, young lady," Ben Senior said, rising on one elbow. Just as quickly, he fell back to the ground.

"Hurry, please. Ask them to call an ambulance."

"No ambulance, son, I mean it!"

"I have my cell phone," she said, reaching for her pocket.

"Won't work out here. Have Ben phone when you reach the house."

Robbie looked over to Emma, his niece near tears. "Hey, sweetie, Grandpa's gonna be fine, sweetie. He just got hot, but you know Grandma. She'll want him checked out by the doctor, okay?"

She nodded. "Now, you show Hope the way back, okay?"

Lips jutted and resolute, the child turned her pony toward home as Hope leaped back on Whimsy .

"We'll be back soon!" she said, gazing from father to son.

"Thanks," Robbie said, marveling again at her ease in the saddle.

*****

In less than five minutes, Ben was back with the cart. Hope and Emma had stayed with baby Ben. By the time the cart reached them, Ben Senior was sitting up, drinking water and chatting. "I'm fine, as you can see," he said in answer to his eldest's query.

Robbie gazed up at his brother. "Looks like heatstroke. Are the EMTs on the way?"

"Yup."

"If you two think I'm goin' to the hospital in an ambulance, you've got another think comin'. Now help me up and let's be on our way."

His eldest gave his father a hand and the elder Morgan rose shakily to his feet, Robbie propping his other side. "Better just surrender now, Dad. Mom's already at the house," Ben said.

He broke free of them and headed for the cart. "No need to have called her. Probably gotten your poor mother all shaken up for a little case of heatstroke!"

The brothers looked at each other. It was the rare occasion when their father expressed anger or irritation at one of his children, and he was clearly furious. Without a word, Ben slipped in beside him and drove off. Robbie followed on Thor.

Ben Senior refused to go in the ambulance, so Leonora and Robbie drove him to his doctor's in town, where he was given IV fluids, pronounced "fit as a fiddle."

"A nap and lots of hydration for the rest of the day. No alcohol," said his good friend and physician, Chester Black, as they said their good-byes.

Ben Senior grinned. "Thanks, buddy. Anything to get these worrywarts off my back."

Leonora rolled her eyes, "Thanks, Chet. Hope to see you and Maisie the Club soon!" She took hold of her husband's arm. "And you're taking a nap after lunch or I'm canceling tonight's dinner."

"If I didn't love you so much, darlin', I'd punch you."

"But you do, my love, so let's go home."

Her arm circled his waist and Ben drew her close, leaning against her just a little as they made their way to her car

CHAPTER 10

"Hope, are you sure you're ready for this?" Beth said, leaning heavily on Lang's arm as they rounded her parents' house and headed up the lawn to the terrace. "There's nothing quite like a Morgan family dinner."

"Except a Morgan family Christmas," her husband said.

"Valley Christmas, you mean," his wife said. "Your parents are no slouches when it comes to the holidays, and I imagine Spark isn't either."

Hope laughed, watching her friend, who despite her joking was clearly uncomfortable.

"Your folks won't miss you back in Tintown?" he asked.

"My mom and stepfather are going to Hawaii."

"Hawaii!" Beth exclaimed.

"They invited me, but I'd much rather be here. Believe me."

Beth stopped, clutching her side.

"Sweetheart, what is it?" Lang asked, eyes full of concern.

"Nothing, just a cramp."

"Cramp? You could be in labor!"

"Relax, sweetie. If it's labor, it's really early labor. You remember they said it could go on for days?"

"That's it. We're going home."

"No, we are not!" She straightened up, holding her belly. "There now, it's gone." Beth put her hand on his wrist. "I'm fine, promise. If anything happens, you'll be the first to know. Now, let's—"

"Beth, Lang, Hope! What are you doing hiding down there?" Leonora Morgan called from the terrace. "Come up and join the party!"

As they climbed the stone steps, the group enveloped them. Beth's parents and their dear friend Spark Foster greeted them first. Spark's daughter, Amy, and her fiancé, Jeb Barnes, were right behind them. Their tiny redheaded son, Toby, rolled up in his wheelchair to say hello, a huge grin on his face.

"Ms. Seymour, Spark Foster! Yer looking well."

Hope had met the Fosters once, at Beth and Lang's wedding. She hadn't imagined he'd remember her. "Hello, Mr. Foster. So nice to see you again. And it's Hope, please."

"Right back at'cha. Everyone calls me Spark and I expect you to follow suit! You've met my daughter, Amy, and her handsome fiancé?"

"Hello. So good to see you both."

Hope hugged Amy. Then Jeb stepped forward and gave her a firm handshake.

"Hey, Hope. Good to see you." Like most of the local cowboys, he was drop-dead handsome, all wiry muscle. He looked vaguely uncomfortable in new jeans and a plaid collared shirt, both appearing to have come right out of the box. "We hope you're going to be here for the wedding?"

"I wouldn't miss it unless the baby comes and I'm babysitting."

"Nonsense. Kids of all ages are comin'," Spark said. "And if they get bored with the festivities, we've got a slew of women to take 'em inside for fun and games, including my fine grandson here. Have you met him?"

"No, hello," Hope said, approaching the frail little boy who was grinning from ear to ear. She reached out her hand and he shook it.

"Hi, miss. Welcome to the Valley. It's awesome!"

Hope smiled. "It sure is! So nice to meet you, Toby. I've heard so much about you."

As Beth stooped to hug the child, Maggie Morgan approached, her son on her hip. "Hello again!"

"Hello, Maggie, hello, Ben," she said, ruffling the child's curls. "Where's your big sister?"

"She went with her daddy to pick up Uncle Kyle at the airport. They should be here soon."

Ben Morgan's wife looked radiant, as always, in a peasant blouse and floral skirt, her ample cleavage on full display as her son tugged at her neckline. "I'm sorry, I'm headed into the house. Someone's hungry and this is the only time of the day when he still nurses."

As Maggie turned toward the house, Jeb said, "I'm gonna get this guy out to the lawn to play with the dogs, but then I'm headed to the bar. Can I get you a drink, Hope? As you'd expect, they have everything. Beer, wine, sodas, and Raoul makes a mean margarita."

"I'd love a margarita. Thanks," Hope said.

Amy and Hope watched Jeb wheel his son off, lift him from his chair, and settle him on a blanket spread on the lawn at the edge of the terrace. The ranch's three Australian shepherds immediately besieged him, knocking Toby over and jumping up on Jeb's new jeans. As the dogs settled beside the child, Jeb brushed off his jeans, ruffled Toby's curls and headed off to the bar.

"Your son's a cutie. Your husband-to-be, too," she said.

Amy gave her a warm smile, tucking a strand of her auburn hair behind her ear. "I'm really lucky. I thought I'd be living and working in Portland forever until Dad dragged me here on a forced vacation, and look where it's taken me."

"You work in Tucson now, don't you?"

She nodded. "Toby's school is two blocks from the clinic. It's worked out really well. Unfortunately, his school is closing in six months, so we're scrambling to find care for him. Jeb's in school now and it's been a bit of a juggling act. My dad's offered to fund my temporary retirement, but I like my work and Toby needs friends and his own space. I'm sure it will work out somehow."

"Here you go, ladies," Jeb said, beer bottle tucked under his arm, as he handed them both huge margaritas.

"Oh, my," Hope said after taking a tangy, salty sip. "Delicious!"

Amy laughed. "And strong. Watch out."

A raven-haired stranger approached, red wine in hand. She looked to be about thirty. "Hope, this is my dad's new cook, Aria Fiorelli," Amy said. Violet eyes studied Hope as the woman reached out and shook her hand.

"So you're new to the Valley, too?" Hope asked as the woman's dead fish handshake slipped away.

"Arrived last week," the other replied, her husky voice somehow managing to sound simultaneously sexy and intimidating. "Spark and I are old friends."

"He's a great guy, your dad," Hope said, turning to Amy.

"Yes, he is."

As the group stood talking, Nick Parker and Harley Langdon strolled in, greeting their hosts, then heading for the bar. "Oh, my," Aria said.

Hope laughed. "Oh, my, indeed. The Valley breeds some gorgeous cowboys, doesn't it?"

Sandy-haired, with the wiry build of the wrangler he was, Langdon stood almost four inches taller than his brown-haired, broad-shouldered assistant.

"Who the hell are they?" Aria asked, eyes never leaving the two cowboys who, beers in hand, were now headed their way.

Hope had met Harley at Beth's wedding, but the other man was a stranger. Before she could answer Aria, Harley said, "Ladies, lads," and raised his beer.

"Hope, you know Harley," Jeb said. "Aria, Harley's my boss. He and Maggie run the stables. And this is Nick Parker, wrangler, trainer, and horse whisperer extraordinaire."

As the two men shook their hands, Amy said, "Where's Willow? I thought she was coming? Toby's been so excited to see her."

"Her mom wanted her home for a few days. She's havin' a poor spell. Cheers her up to have Willow around."

"I'm sure it does," Amy said. "Aria, Willow's Harley's daughter."

"How old?" Aria asked, moving closer to the tall, handsome cowboy.

"Fifteen." He gazed down, studying the newcomer, a wry smile playing in his green eyes. *We've got a live wire here,* he mused. "What brings you to the Valley, Ms. Fiorelli?"

"It's Aria, hon. I'm with Spark?"

"Oh?" Harley gazed from Aria to Amy.

Before Amy could respond, Aria laughed. "His chef. We worked together in Portland."

Amy watched her dad's chef, wondering at her behavior. It was a side of her she had never seen before, and Aria had been working for her dad for several years.

At that moment, Robbie Morgan stepped onto the terrace, a case of beer under one arm, bags of ice in each hand. Hope's heart skipped as she watched him confer with Raoul over the cooler. Someone else had not missed his arrival. She looked sideways to find Aria Fiorelli practically salivating. Robbie loaded the cooler and grabbed a beer, then strolled off, nodding to Spark and his parents as he passed them.

"Hey, guys, ladies," he said, noticing the dark-haired stranger. *Who could miss her?* But Hope's nearness took his breath away. No woman had ever had this effect on him. She looked lovely in a thin sleeveless top, its neckline revealing a hint of her rounded breasts, her black pencil skirt hugging every inch of her lithe, lean body. *And those legs, strong, slender and perfect!*

Amy watched the usually cool, confident Morgan brother turning to mush at the sight of Hope and smiled. *When the right woman comes along, even the Morgan brothers fall.* "Hi, Robbie. I don't think you've met Aria Fiorelli, my dad's new cook."

"Aria," he said, nodding to the violet-eyed beauty. *And she is beautiful. A young Liz Taylor. Any other time and I'd be there.* "Great to meet you."

"I'm a chef, not a cook, and the pleasure's all mine, cowboy," she said, leaning toward him, limp hand extended, Nick and Harley forgotten.

Hope watched Robbie's reaction to Aria's flirting, marveling at his poise and surprised not to see him turn on the Morgan charm. Handsome as always, he wore a green sport shirt that picked up the color in his soft eyes. His jeans hung just right on his tight, athletic frame. *Good enough to eat* came to mind, and at that moment it looked as though Spark's new chef intended to do just that. Hope took a huge swig of her margarita and scanned the group, wondering how Beth was doing. She spied her friend sitting on a wicker love seat, Lang at her side, fussing.

"Excuse me," she said to no one in particular, crossing the terrace quickly.

"I'm fine, really," Beth said as Hope arrived beside them. "Hope, please distract him! He's driving me so crazy that I'm tempted to order a strong margarita."

"Probably wouldn't hurt at this point," Maggie said, coming to sit beside her. "Go on and get a drink, father-to-be. We'll hover for a while."

Hope sat in a chair next to the two and took another sip of her drink.

"Oh, that looks delicious," Beth said. Hope passed the glass and she took a very small sip. "Thanks, I needed that." She held her belly, gazing across the terrace. "I see Aria, 'I'm a chef, not a cook,' is making friends."

Hope laughed. "She seems very taken with your brother."

"From what I hear, she's very taken with anyone in pants. I hope Spark knows what he's getting into."

"I talked to Spark earlier," Maggie said. "Apparently she's an amazing chef and very loyal to him. I suspect most of it's an act."

"Maybe," Hope said, voice trailing off as she looked up in time to see Aria's hand reach around to rub Robbie's shoulder. He made no move to step away.

Beth winked at Maggie as they watched her friend. *She's crazy about him and there's not a damn thing I can do about it except watch another one of my brothers break a woman's heart.*

"You okay?" Maggie asked, noticing Beth wince.

"Just a little pang. Uh-oh," she added, looking toward the terrace door as her two brothers and Emma stepped out. "Here comes trouble, Emma excluded, of course."

Chapter 11

"Kyle, honey, finally!" Leonora Morgan cried, rushing to greet her fifth child, a slimmer, shorter version of his oldest brother who followed him, Emma in his arms.

"Grandpa! We're back," Emma cried, hopping down and running into his open arms. "Are you feeling better?"

"Right as rain, sweetheart, and ready for some tag. Where are those dogs, anyway?"

Leonora frowned. "Ben, you promised."

"I promised to take it easy, and I will. Now, Em, let's get yer brother and head down to join Toby and the pups, shall we?"

"He's okay, Mom," Ben said, hugging Maggie as the baby wriggled from her arms and toddled after his sister and grandfather. "It's not like he's gonna run a marathon. Where's their partner in crime, by the way?"

"You know Ruthie. She took that man into town so she's late, of course. Always has to be difficult!"

You have no idea, Ben thought. With his father's collapse, he had not had time to catch his sister for a chat. *Hope Dad doesn't have a heart attack.*

As if on cue, Ruthie and Kevin strolled around from the side yard and joined the melee on the lawn, dogs barking and children squealing. Ben noticed that his father was sitting on the wall, observing, and breathed a sigh.

As usual, Carmela outdid herself. Two long tables fully set with Leonora's colorful pottery and linens now held platters of food. Skewers of beef, chicken, lamb, cilantro-infused trout, and shrimp. There was also a platter of her signature dish, grilled portabellas, Ben Morgan the son's favorite dish. Stuffed peppers with quinoa and black beans, Mexican pasta with vegetables and chili, sweet potato bean salads, and huge bowls of green salad lined the table along with baskets of cornbread and Carmela's homemade tortillas, salsa, and guacamole.

Kyle grinned. "Oh, my God—I've been dreaming of this for months, Carm. They don't make food like this in Boston."

"Or anywhere, for that matter," Spark Foster said, coming from behind to pat his back. "Good to see you, son. How's the veterinarian trade?"

"Wild and woolly. Hey, Spark, great to see you. Lookin' forward to the big wedding. Ben tells me you've brought your own cook from Portland."

"Yup, Aria's a keeper. Been workin' for me for years." He leaned over and winked. "She prefers 'chef,' I believe." As he spoke, he glanced at his newest employee now draped on Robbie Morgan's shoulder at the bar and laughed. "Looks like she's made a friend."

"That's your chef?"

"The very one."

"Looks like my brother's turned on the charm."

"Dinner is served," Leonora called clapping her hands. "Fill your drinks and find a spot!"

As her guests found seats, Leonora spied her youngest arm in arm with her boyfriend, Kevin Statler. Leonora frowned as her husband's arm circled her tiny waist. "Now, Nora, he's a nice enough boy. Leave her be. We all know who she's gonna end up with. These are her wild oats."

"If you're referring to Harley Langdon, I'm not sure I like that any better. Come on, then. Let's go say hello."

Leonora bore down on the pair, waving. "Ruthie, Kevin, yoo-hoo, sorry we didn't see you come in. Get yourself drink and find a seat. Don't want Carmela's food getting cold. Kevin, nice to see you again, dear." She hugged the startled young man, who looked out of place and uncomfortable in starched khakis and an oxford shirt. His dirty-blond hair was windblown and longish. His pale brown eyes darted around the terrace.

Scared rabbit, Ben Senior mused. "Good to have you, son. I'm sure there are a few people you don't know, but Ruthie can introduce you. It's a friendly crowd."

"Thanks, Mr. Morgan."

"Ben, if you please. No Mr. Morgans around here. Have you met my buddy, Spark Foster?"

"I don't think so."

"Well here he is. Spark, come meet Ruthie's friend, Kevin Statler."

"The prettiest redhead this side of the mountains," Spark said, giving Ruthie a hug, then turning to her companion. "Good to meet you, son."

"Hello, sir."

"None of that now. It's Spark. Now go along and join the young ones. We old codgers gotta find a seat."

Ben Senior noticed his usually loquacious daughter had barely spoken a word. She gave her father a nod and a smile and guided Kevin toward the bar. As Ruthie handed Kevin a beer, Kyle caught her up in a bear hug, then shook Kevin's hand. "Nice to meet you, buddy."

Hope headed for Beth and Lang, who encouraged her to sit with them. As they filled their plates, she spied Aria Fiorelli and Robbie on the other side of the table. *She's made her conquest. No need to concern myself about Robbie Morgan. He'll be otherwise occupied until he returns to Sedona. Thank goodness!* She told herself this development was a relief, but she felt sad and lonely as she followed her friends.

Chapter 12

They took seats near Beth's dad and Spark, who sat at one end of a long table, Leonora at the other end. "Sorry not to see your folks tonight," Spark said to Lang.

"Yeah, Dad wasn't feeling great and Mom didn't want to leave him. They're looking forward to the wedding, though."

"Aren't we all?"

"Is Aria doing all the catering?"

Spark chuckled. "Let's just say she's in charge. She's got a whole crew comin' from Portland and she's hired some locals, too."

"Son, come join us," Ben Senior said, waving to Robbie, who had a full plate and had managed to extract himself from Aria. The new chef had set her plate down beside Nick Parker at the other table, then headed to the bar, obviously expecting Robbie to take the empty seat on the other side of her. She was not pleased when she saw him take the remaining empty seat at the opposite table, beside Hope Seymour.

"Thanks, Dad." He nodded to Hope, brushing her arm as he sat down.

His touch and nearness sent treacherous shivers through her, and Hope sat up straight and moved a few inches away.

Robbie breathed a sigh of relief. Thanks to his dad, he had escaped from Aria, the barracuda. He felt at home sitting next to Hope, Lang, and Beth, and he always enjoyed the company of his father and Spark. Almost without thinking, he reached down and took her hand.

Surprised, Hope turned beet red and withdrew her hand, but not before feeling a warm flush coursing through her body. She looked up to see Beth staring at her, concern in her eyes. "You okay?" she whispered, having seen her brother's less-than-subtle move.

Hope nodded. "Of course. You're the one who's in labor," she whispered.

"Don't tell Lang, but I'm getting regular contractions now. It's gonna be tonight. I'm pretty sure."

Robbie felt like a fool. His impulsive gesture had backfired and now Hope was giving him the cold shoulder, whispering with Beth. He was hard as a rock and glad of his mother's oversized linen napkin in his lap.

"Don't you think you should go to the hospital now?" Hope whispered.

"Soon. I'm not eating more than a mouthful."

Hope squeezed her friend's hand, then turned her attention to the incredible food in front of her. She loved cooking and was an excellent cook, but living alone, she rarely made the effort, instead existing on prepared foods and simple meals that could be whipped up in five to ten minutes. This was heaven, every succulent bite.

As she tried without much success to ignore Robbie's presence, she listened to the two old friends talking about the upcoming wedding. It was to be held on New Year's Eve with a dinner, then dancing until the new year dawned. Spark Foster, a self-made billionaire, did nothing halfway, according to Beth, so Hope imagined it would be a spectacular day and evening. She was also looking forward to seeing the new house designed by Sam Morgan.

"Yup, the troops arrive a couple days before. Aria's got a dozen or so coming in, and then I have a crew coming to do the fireworks. Should be somethin' the whole Valley can enjoy," he said, grinning widely.

"You always were a showman," Ben Senior said. "Patsy would be thrilled and proud."

"Yes, she would," Spark said, eyes sad at the mention of his wife, who had passed away several years earlier. "My Pats loved fireworks and she sure loved a good party. Only hope I can live up to her standards. Don't know what I'd do without your Nora. Bet you'll be glad to have her back. She's been over with us night and day."

"She loves it every minute. Keeps her outta my hair." He winked at his friend. "You know I love her more each day, but she's a mother hen if there ever was one."

"As well she should be. How're ya feelin'?"

"Fit as a fiddle. Can't have a bit of heatstroke without callin' out the army. How's your pretty cook settlin' in?"

"Great. Her apartment's all furnished and she's already running everyone in sight. In fact," he said, leaning toward his friend. "there have been a couple of skirmishes between her and your Nora."

Ben Senior chuckled. "I'll just bet there have. I'm sure there'll be more ahead, too. My advice—stay out of the line of fire."

"Robbie, my boy," Spark said, a twinkle in his eye. "My new chef seemed quite taken with you."

Ben Senior watched his son blanch and the cheeks of the lovely woman beside him turn bright red. *There is something going on with those two*, he mused, his eyes scanning the table to the far end where Leonora was holding court, Maggie, Ben, and the children around her. Ruthie and her date were in the middle, Kevin appearing ill at ease beside the baby. Ruthie sat across the table beside Emma, the two chattering away as usual. *Wish Sam was here.* Harley, Jeb, Amy, Toby, and Nick Parker sat at the other table with Aria now glued to Nick. *She's trouble*, the ranch patriarch thought. *Half the Valley men'll be turned upside down and inside out by New Year's.*

"Beth, are you okay?" his son-in-law asked, drawing his attention back to his immediate companions.

His eldest daughter waved her hand and said, "I'm fine," but she did not look fine.

"Sweetheart, why don't you go in the house and lie down? Carmela can get you something."

"Thanks, Dad, but I'm okay."

At that moment, their attention was diverted by the hostess, who rose from her chair and motioned to her husband. He stood and walked the length of the table to stand by her side. Leonora then clinked her wineglass and said, "Attention everyone! Ben and I have an announcement that we hope will be happy news."

As all eyes turned to her, Robbie leaned back and whispered, "Hope, I'm sorry about the hand thing. Don't know what I was thinking."

"No problem," she said, giving him a tight smile as she turned her attention to their hosts.

"We have been truly blessed," Ben Senior said, "in our children and now our grandchildren. With more on the way and our new grandnephew, Toby," he said, winking at the child and his parents at the next table.

"And despite our best efforts, our offspring and their spouses insist upon working," Leonora continued. Her son Ben opened his mouth to speak, but she waved her hand. "Never mind, Benny. I've accepted that this is the modern way. This is not about that."

"It's about doing our part as grandparents," her husband said. "So, we've decided to expand the ranch's properties. The Slocum cottage on the west end of town was gonna be demolished. Seemed a terrible shame. It's a beautiful building, quite recently restored, lots of possibilities."

"For what?" his son Ben asked, unable to contain his curiosity. *As the ranch's manager, I should have been informed!*

"For a nursery, day care!" she said, clapping her hands. "We've bought the cottage and will have it moved to the ranch as soon as we all decide on the right spot."

Ben Senior gazed around at all the surprised faces. "We have some ideas for location, but the property is as much yours as ours now, so we wanted you all to decide on where to plunk it down." His arm circled his wife's shoulders. "Soon as it's moved and sited, we'll begin renovations with our family architect's help, of course. When it's ready for business, we'll hire the best caregivers we can find, including helpers for Toby." He winked at Spark, who was clearly in on the plan.

"That'll be his granddaddy's project," Spark said, smiling across to Amy and Jeb, whose jaws had practically hit the tabletop.

"I don't believe it!" Maggie said.

"Just sorry your father couldn't be here tonight. He has some suggestions, too, darlin'." Ben Senior smiled at his daughter-in-law. "Course our Emma is in school now, but she'll be over to help run the place after school, won't you sweetie?"

"Sure will, Grandpa!"

Leonora waved her hands. "Enough for now. Everyone enjoy your dinner! Carmela has some incredible desserts she's laying out as we speak. Help yourselves, please."

Ben Senior kissed his wife on the temple and headed back to his place at the table. He had barely taken his seat when Ruthie popped up.

Chapter 13

"I have an announcement, too," the youngest Morgan said, cheeks red, chin jutted out. I mean, Kevin and I have an announcement."

Leonora Morgan eyed her youngest sharply but said nothing as Ruthie motioned to Kevin to stand. He looked as if he was bracing himself for a root canal.

"Kev and I are so excited to tell you all that we're engaged!"

"What?"

"That's right, Mama. Your baby's getting married."

"Don't be ridiculous, Ruthie Ann. This is neither the time nor the place."

"It certainly is!" Ruthie said, cheeks aflame now as she glared at her mother. "We love each other and we're getting married this spring. We haven't set the date, but we will this week while we're camping."

"Camping?" Leonora exclaimed, voice shrill. "Did you know about this?" she asked, gazing down the table to her husband. As the family patriarch shrugged and shook his head, he caught a glimpse of Harley at the next table. His face had turned ashen, a mirror reflection of the shock they all felt.

Leonora waved her hand. "It's a week before Christmas, for goodness' sakes! No one goes off camping the week before Christmas!"

"Well, we do, and we are. We're leaving Monday morning and that's that."

"I absolutely forbid it!"

"Nora, honey, let everyone get their desserts and then we'll raise a glass to Ruthie and Kevin."

"We certainly will not! Why, I—"

"Oh, Lang, look!" Beth cried, gazing downward.

Always their quiet child, both parents stared in disbelief at their oldest daughter, who had never raised her voice at a family dinner.

"My water's broken!"

Without a word, Lang stood and scooped her up in his arms as if she were light as a feather. Robbie hopped up, too. "I'll drive."

"I'm coming, too," Hope said, following the three as they headed for the terrace steps.

"Take your mom's car," Ben Senior called to his son. "Keys are under the mat."

CHAPTER 14

They settled Beth into the Volvo's backseat, Lang beside her, and the other two hopped into the front. Beth was moaning now and clearly in pain. Hope turned to him. "How far is the hospital?"

"Twenty minutes tops," Lang said. "Less if you hit the floor and don't let up."

Robbie peeled out as Lang pulled out his phone and called the midwife.

"It's okay, sweetie," he said as he hung up. "She's on her way. Will be there before we are."

"If the baby waits that long," she said, gasping as another contraction hit.

"Breathe, baby, breathe," he said. "Hee, hah, hee hah."

"Stop it, Lang! Your beer breath is making me want to throw up!"

"Transition," he said. "She's right. We may not make it. Anyone got a breath mint?"

Hope pulled a cough lozenge from her purse and handed it to Lang. "This might help. Have either of you got any medical training?"

"Not for this," Robbie said. "We'll make it. Don't worry, sis."

They sped along the dark highway in silence except for Beth's moans and Lang's coaching. He rubbed her back and made soothing sounds, although they appeared largely ineffectual. As they neared the turnoff for Valley Hospital, Beth screamed, "Stop the car! The baby's coming now!"

"Sweetie, hold on. It's only five minutes. Breathe. Don't push."

"I can't help it!"

"There's a parking lot up ahead," Robbie said. "What d'you want me to do?"

"Drive on. She can make it, can't you sweetie? Beth? Beth? What is it? Wake up!"

"What's happening?" Hope snapped off her seat belt and jumped up to peer into the backseat.

"She's lost consciousness. Oh, God, Beth!" Lang cried, holding her.

Hope grabbed a water bottle from the floor and wet the sleeve of her sweater, passing it back to him. "Put this on her forehead."

"We're here!" Robbie shouted, turning into the well-lit hospital entrance and parking at the emergency room doors. He jumped out and rushed in, grabbing the first nurse he saw. "Pregnant woman in labor. She's unconscious and needs immediate help. Now!"

Before they could roll out the gurney, Lang appeared through the double doors, Beth in his arms, shouting. "She's Kathy Myers's patient. Kathy should be waiting for us."

"She's going to the OR," the nurse said, settling Beth on a gurney. "We'll page your mid-wife have her meet us there."

Car forgotten, Hope and Robbie followed Beth's gurney, Lang at Beth's side, holding her hand. When they reached the second floor operating room area, the nurse turned to him. "We'll take her from here, sir. I'm sure Kathy Myers will come out to get you as soon as she can."

"No, I'm coming with her."

"I'm sorry, Mr. Dillon, but you cannot. Please let go of the gurney. We need to get her in there."

After one last look at his beloved sister, white as a ghost and drenched in sweat, Robbie turned to his brother-in-law and grabbed his arm. "Come on, buddy. Let 'em take care of her. I'm as scared as you are, but she's gonna be fine. Let her go."

Tears in his eyes, Lang allowed himself to be led to a small waiting area at the end of the hall. The two men sat, Lang's head between his knees. Robbie looked up at Hope, and she saw that he, too, was crying. "Why don't I find us some coffee," she said softly. "Or water? I'll check on the car, too."

Shaken to the core, she headed for the elevator. *Please, please let her be okay,* she thought as the doors closed behind her.

CHAPTER 15

When she returned with a carrier full of coffees and waters, she found Lang in the same position and Robbie pacing. "Any word from the doctors?"

"Not a peep," Robbie said, accepting the coffee she handed him.

"Lang," she said softly. "Would you like anything?"

In a daze, Beth's husband looked up at her as if she were a stranger. "Thanks," he said, taking a water bottle. His hair was disheveled, eyes red and swollen, face flushed. "Why haven't they come out?"

"They will soon, buddy." Robbie sat down beside him, patting his shoulder.

"I'm giving them ten minutes. Then I'm going in. Don't you see? I promised her I wouldn't leave her."

"She knows you're here," Robbie said, thinking how useless his reassurances sounded.

Hope sat on the other side of Lang, every so often gazing at Robbie, who looked almost as defeated and scared as his brother-in-law.

A door closed down the hall, and she looked up. Here comes someone."

"Kathy, thank God," Lang said, leaping out of his seat to meet the midwife, who looked exhausted.

"She's stable."

"And the baby?"

"You have a beautiful baby girl," Kathy said, giving him a weary smile as she squeezed his forearm.

"Thank God. Can I see them?"

"Not yet. They're still working on Beth and the baby, too."

"What's wrong?"

"We had to take the baby by an emergency cesarean. Baby's okay, just groggy with the aftermath of labor. She was partially down the birth canal when we pulled her back and out. Beth's lost a lot of blood. She had pre-eclampsia. She must've been in labor for a while and should have come in sooner."

Lang held the midwife's arm in a death grip. "We tried, believe me. Is she going to be okay? Please, I have to see her."

"The doctors won't allow it. She's stable, but not out of the woods. As soon as they finish with your daughter, I'll bring her out," she said, gently trying to extract herself from his grip. "She's got the best doctors in the hospital taking care of her. Hold tight, okay? I'd like to go back in now."

Robbie stepped forward, taking hold of Lang's arm. "Let her go, bro, so she can get back to Beth."

Lang let go of her arm. "Please, Kathy, I need to be with her."

"I'll try. I promise."

Hope led him back to sit while Robbie walked down the hall with the midwife. "Tell me the truth. Is my sister going to pull through this?"

"Her condition is still critical, but she's young and she's strong. Right now they worry about the damage from the stroke."

"Stroke?"

"Yes, that's why she lost consciousness."

"Jesus Christ," he muttered.

"They're doing everything they can," Kathy Myers said. "I'll be back as soon as I can."

Chapter 16

After what seemed like an eternity, in reality about fifteen minutes, Kathy Myers appeared, holding a tiny pink bundle. "Here she is," she said, handing the baby to Lang.

"Oh, Lang, she's beautiful!" Hope exclaimed, gazing down at the tiny little face with rosy pink cheeks and a tuft of dark hair.

"Sure is," Robbie said, clapping Lang on the shoulder. "And my sister?"

"She's awake, but heavily sedated."

"Can I see her?" Lang said, looking up from the baby to the midwife.

"Yes, but only for a few minutes."

"Go on, buddy," Robbie said, patting him on the back. "Tell her we love her. We'll be right here."

Lang, Myers, and the baby disappeared, and Robbie and Hope were left standing side by side in the middle of the empty room. After several seconds, they turned to each other and he reached out his arms. "Thank God," he whispered as they embraced, holding on for dear life. "And thank you so much for being here."

"Sounds like good news," she said, rubbing his back, not wanting to let go.

He stepped back slightly, arms still encircling her. "She's had a stroke. Kathy didn't say what the effects or damage were."

Hope blanched. "Oh, Robbie." She reached up and stroked his cheek. Then, in the middle of that stark, cold room, he drew her close and kissed her, craving her warmth and comfort. Despite her vows to keep her distance, Hope responded as the kiss grew deeper. It was as if their longing for one another mingled with their worry about Beth and fused them as one being for those few seconds.

Suddenly remembering where they were, Robbie pulled back. "Sorry, I've done it again, haven't I?"

She gave him a wry smile and said, "Under the circumstances, I think it was a good move, but maybe we should sit down?"

They sat side by side, his arm around her shoulders as Hope leaned against him. Neither wanted to relinquish the warmth and comfort of the other's touch. That was how Lang found them a few minutes later.

"She's in pretty rough shape, but they say she's gonna be fine. She had a small stroke due to a sudden rise in her blood pressure, but it seems to have left only a slight weakness in her left arm. She hasn't been running around the room, but they don't think it affected her legs."

"Thank God," Robbie said, standing and hugging his brother-in-law.

Hope embraced him. "So glad, Lang. So glad."

"Thanks. Me, too. You two go home. I'm going to stay with her tonight."

"Are you sure?" Robbie asked. "We can camp out here, too."

"No, and please tell everyone that she's okay and to wait until morning to come."

"Already called 'em, brother."

"Is there anything you or Beth need?" Hope asked. "I could gather clothes for her and Robbie could get some things for you."

"Actually, that'd be great in the morning. Thanks. For now, we're fine. They gave me a toothbrush and a cot so I'll survive till then. We're going up to the third floor, room 367. Thanks again for everything. I owe you big time. Not sure we'd have made it without you."

Lang embraced them both and said good night.

Chapter 17

Both exhausted, Robbie and Hope rode back to the ranch in silence, before stepping into the barrage of questions from his parents and siblings. Maggie had taken the kids home and the stable crew had departed, but Ruthie, Kevin, Kyle, and Martha Dillon joined them in the living room for a recounting of Beth's condition and the birth. Lang's mother had rushed over when Leonora called and was now wondering if she should head to the hospital. Robbie persuaded her that waiting until morning was what her son wanted, so she sat back.

"I fear Bethie has inherited my disposition to high blood pressure at the tail end of pregnancy," Leonora said, wringing her hands. "I cannot believe that midwife of hers didn't catch it, especially since the baby was overdue."

"Now, Nora, we don't know the circumstances," her husband said.

"If she'd only seen a doctor. Doctors don't miss things like that."

"Actually, they do, Mama," Ruthie said. "Maybe it just cropped up at the end?"

"And you would know because?" her oldest brother said.

"Because I was a premed biology major, as you well know."

"That's enough from you tonight, Ruthie," her mother said. "Oh, I can't wait to see our granddaughter. I'll bet she's a little doll."

"She is very cute," Hope said, smiling wearily.

"You look tired, darlin'," Ben Senior said. "Can we fix you up a bed here so you don't go home to an empty house?"

"Thank you so much, but I'll be fine. I won't say no to a ride home, though."

Ben opened his mouth to offer, but Robbie beat him to it. "I'll take you."

"Thanks. That'd be great."

As his wife bustled about, shooing them out the door, Ben Senior watched the interplay between the two, convinced there was something going on, a palpable connection between his son and Beth's enigmatic friend.

They said their good nights and walked out with Ben. The eldest Morgan son paused beside his Rover. "Night, brother, Hope. Sounds like you two saved our sister's life. I predict that tonight will be the last moment of peace those two have for a good long time."

They drove Leonora's car up to the darkened house and both hopped out. "You have a key?" he asked.

Hope laughed. "On my dresser, in my room."

"We'll find a way. In fact, I bet the door's open." The front door was locked. The kitchen door was not. "Voila!" he said, swinging it open, then reaching for a light switch.

Suddenly shy and acutely aware that they were alone together, she said, "Thanks for the ride. You must be exhausted, too."

He smiled, locking the kitchen door and following her to the front door nearest the driveway. When they reached the door, he said, "Truth is, I'd like nothing better than to carry you up those stairs and make wild, passionate love to you, but that's a horny man talking. That's *not* what you want."

"I'm honestly not sure what I want," she lied. *Wild passionate sex with you is exactly what I want.*

"Well, I won't push, but I'd love to take you to dinner sometime this week before the holiday craziness—that is, when Beth and Lang don't need you. If dinner's too much, we could take a ride and have lunch. Anything. What do you think?"

"I'm assuming we'll be needed at the farm, or me here during the day, but dinner would be fine. Yes."

"Why don't I head over here about nine tomorrow and we can collect some things for the new parents? We can figure out a good night after talking to them and seeing how long the hospital will be keeping Beth."

"Great. I'll see you in the morning."

He started to open the door.

"Robbie?"

He turned back, and Hope leaned forward and kissed him, her arms circling his broad, strong shoulders. Their mouths opened and tongues delved deep, teasing, caressing, entwining. Robbie drew her to him and she felt his erection hard against her belly. *Stop while you can, Hope, or there'll be no stopping!*

Breathless, she pulled away. "Good night," she murmured, giving him a shy smile.

"So it's official—you really are trying to kill me."

"No, but it's late and reason has prevailed."

Never know it from your behavior! "Damn reason… Okay, night, then." He kissed her forehead and stepped outside, breathing the cool night air to calm his seething libido. *Not sure where this is headed, but I'm sure looking forward to the trip!*

Hope leaned against the closed door, still breathless and light-headed. *What have I done?* she thought before heading up the stairs on wobbly knees.

CHAPTER 18

True to his word, Robbie arrived at the house shortly before nine. Hope was in the kitchen, drinking a cup tea. A bag for Beth sat on the front porch. She had dressed deliberately for comfort and confidence in jeans and her favorite casual sweater. A pale blue, it picked up the color of her eyes, and it hugged her thin frame in all the right places. Her hair was in two long braids. *Here goes,* she thought, heading to the front door.

"Mornin'," he said, giving her one of his high-wattage smiles. "Sleep well?"

"Yes, thanks. You?"

"Like a baby. Truth is, I always sleep well at home. It's the ranch sounds, or lack of sounds, I think."

He wore jeans, a faded gray ranch tee shirt, and a well-broken-in leather jacket. *If he looked any sexier, I'd be forced to throw myself at him right on this front porch!* "It is peaceful here," she said. "Come in. I've got Beth's things and found a duffle bag for you to use for Lang's. It's on their bed. Have you eaten?"

"Yup, all set. I'll head up, then. You look great, by the way," he said. *Great? Who am I kidding? Great doesn't even come close.*

As they drove to the hospital, they were all business, talking about the ranch and upcoming holidays. Both were slated to help out at the farm, Robbie most days and Hope unless Beth needed her.

"I'm happy to help at the farm," she said. "I doubt my nannying duties will kick in for a few weeks. I imagine the new parents will want to take care of the baby. Besides, your mom and Lang's have stocked their fridge and freezer for at least a month, so they don't need me to cook."

He laughed. "You mean Carmela and the Dillons' cook, Jon, have stocked the larder. Mom barely remembers how to boil an egg. Don't you want to use your free time to paint?"

Her face paled and Hope gazed straight ahead at the mountains in the distance. "Truth is, I'm happy for a break from it. I brought everything with me and I will get back to it in a month or so, but right now physical labor and the outdoors are much more appealing."

"Well, you'll get plenty of those," he said, wondering what was behind the change in her demeanor.

CHAPTER 19

When they arrived, they found the third floor of the small hospital overrun by Morgans and Dillons. Kyle, Ruthie, and Robbie's parents stood in the hallway, chatting, Jay Dillon in a chair beside them. Before they could greet the others, Martha Dillion stepped out of Beth's room, giving each a hug. "Oh, thank goodness for you two! Have you seen her yet, my sweet granddaughter?"

"Just a peek last night. She's a beauty," Hope said. "How's Beth doing?"

"Better, but she's very tired and weak. Lang's been taking care of the baby."

"Has your little beauty got a name?" Robbie asked.

"Lily, after my mother. Lily Leonora Dillon."

Hope thought she detected a hint of disappointment in Martha's tone with the baby's middle name her maternal grandmother's rather than her own.

"We brought clothes and things for them," she said, holding up her duffle.

"Good, I'll take them."

"Can we peek in and see my sister?" Robbie asked, stepping toward the door.

"Yes, of course, dear, but be quick. She's very tired."

Robbie and Hope stepped into the room to find Beth dozing and Lang in a recliner, Lily sleeping on his chest. He gave them a weary smile and raised his fingers to his lips. "Both sleeping."

Because it was a double-size room, of which Valley Hospital had several, there was a sitting area separated from the sleeping area and bath. Lang rose, settled the baby in a small bassinet beside the bed, then led them into the sitting area.

"Brought you some gear," Robbie whispered, handing him the duffle. Hope set Beth's bag beside it.

"Thanks, guys. Be good to shower and change clothes. I'm sure one or both of the moms will be only too happy to stay with Beth and Lily."

"How's Beth doing?" Hope asked.

"Pretty good, but they want to keep her at least two, probably three days. She regained feeling in her arm, but she lost a lot of blood. She's been through the wringer. She's also having trouble nursing, which has her in a state. Maggie's coming in later to help there."

Hope placed a hand on his forearm. "What can we do? Please give me some household chores and anything,"

"Thanks. We're in good shape. The Rambler Sports business can carry on without me, although I'll probably check in at the office tomorrow. Depends on how Beth feels. And the house takes care of itself. I asked our housekeeper, Josie to come two days instead of one, so she'll be there to clean on Tuesdays and Thursdays. And as you've observed, our moms have brought enough food for a year and are now threatening to buy us a freezer so they can bring more. Your dad said you're both helping out at the farm. That's really generous of you. I know it sets Beth's mind at ease, especially with Ruthie going away."

"No problem, brother," Robbie said. "I went over everything with Beth last week."

"Are you okay, Lang?" Hope asked, surprised to see Lang so sober.

Tears filled his eyes. "I almost lost her. I don't know what I'd have done. I finally find the love of my life and am happier than any man deserves to be. That could have all been taken away last night, you know?"

Hope reached over so hug him. "But it wasn't. Your beautiful wife and baby are safe and healthy."

Robbie watched as his brother-in-law broke down in sobs, leaning on Hope. After several minutes, they heard the door open, and Leonora and Martha Dillon came in. Robbie hopped up and went to meet them, giving Lang time to collect himself.

"Good, she's sleeping," his mother whispered. "That precious baby, too. Is Lang okay?"

"Yup, just tired and worried about Beth."

"She's gonna be fine," Leonora said. "My Bethie is the strongest of all of you."

"You're right there, Ma. Hope and I'll take off and let them all rest. Lang could use a nap. We brought clothes and things for both of them, so I bet he'd also appreciate a shower."

"Don't you worry, sweetie. Martha and I'll take care of them. I'm sending your father home with Kyle and your sister, too."

A quick wave to Lang, and they joined the hallway crowd. "Hey, guys, we're takin' off. Anyone need a ride?"

"I'll take Dad. We've got a couple of errands in town," Kyle said.

"Then I'll go with you," Ruthie said, hopping up. "Gotta finish packing."

After leaving Ruthie at the big house, Robbie headed for Beth and Lang's. As he drove up to the house, he asked Hope, "You goin' up to the farm?"

She nodded. "Soon as I change clothes."

"Want me to wait and take you?"

"Thanks, but I've got a few things to do. I'll see you there."

"How about Tuesday?"

"Excuse me?"

"Would Tuesday work for dinner?"

She gazed over, smiling shyly. "Tuesday would be perfect."

Chapter 20

As Robbie descended the stairs Monday morning, he heard his mother's shrill voice.

"Ruthie Ann, your father and I absolutely forbid you to go on this trip!"

"Well, we're going and you can't stop us. Kevin'll be here in a few minutes. Robbie and Hope are helping at the farm and I haven't had time off for six months. Besides, no one here cares what we do and you've been nothing but hurtful about my engagement."

"Now, honey, that's not so," her father said. "Was just a bit of a shock, that's all."

"That's the understanding of the century!" Leonora said, hands on hips, spying her son as he stepped into the dining room. "Good morning, darling. What can Carmela get for your breakfast?"

" Mom," he said, eying the buffet on the sideboard as he headed for the kitchen door. "I'll just grab some juice and be right back."

"And when you return, you can help us talk some sense into your sister!"

"Now, Nora."

"Don't 'now Nora' me. I blame you for this, you know. Always spoiling and indulging her."

"That's my cue," Ruthie said, hopping up and kissing her father. "Robbie, see you Wednesday. Mom, Dad, I'm off. Picking up Kev in town."

"What?"

"Mom, do you really think he'd want to come here after your performance Saturday night?"

With that, she stalked out, leaving the others staring open-mouthed.

"Go after her, Ben," Leonora said.

"Let her be, sweetie. Three days to cool off might be the best thing for everyone."

"I agree, Mom."

"Of course you do," she said, throwing up her hands.

His father shrugged.

"Where's Kyle? I'm surprised he hasn't volunteered for farm duty."

"He's with Ned Williams, making the rounds this week. We're so short on veterinarians in the Valley that he's agreed to visit all the ranches while he's here. He may be able to help at the farm later in the week."

Robbie grabbed a plate and filled it with eggs, bacon, and Carmela's Southwestern hash browns. As he sat beside his mother, he saw she was crying. "Mom, Ruthie's gonna be fine. This is just her being Ruthie. We all know who she'll marry someday."

"I do not find that comforting at the moment." She sniffed. "Although I'd like to give Harley Langdon a smack for leading her on for so long."

"Hey, you can't blame Harley. Ruthie's a—"

"Never mind, son," his father said. "Let it be. He's right, though, darlin'. Our baby's gonna be just fine. Let her sow some wild oats and she'll settle down."

Leonora stood up, tossing her napkin on the table. "Excuse my expression, but you two are full of horseshit!"

As she disappeared into the kitchen, Robbie gazed over at his dad. "Should I go see if she's okay?"

"Leave it. She's just worried. I am too. Don't like this camping trip at this time of year, but we can't stop her."

"Ruthie can take care of herself. She's the best rider among us and she knows the mountains better than anyone except Harley."

"Who is much the better rider, if we're bein' honest."

"I meant this family."

"I know, son. Now enjoy your breakfast before it gets cold."

CHAPTER 21

While they were both at the farm for the day, Robbie and Hope barely saw each other as he was helping Raoul and his men with the animals and Hope was picking winter fruits and vegetables. At the end of the day, they met in the farm office and he said, "Want a drink or something before you head back?" Even with her face smudged with dirt and grime, her faded jeans filthy and her hair somewhat scraggly poking out of a baseball cap, she was so beautiful.

She gazed at him with soft eyes. "What did you have in mind? Not sure I have the energy to lift a bottle or glass."

"Beer? Water? They have a fridge in here."

"Beer, thanks. Then I'll go home, shower, and pass out."

Beers in hand, they sat side by side in the shade of the porch behind the office. He smelled of animals and the fields, his strong, tanned arms covered with a thin layer of dust and grime. *Even now, sweaty and covered with dirt, I'd jump into his arms in a heartbeat,* she thought as they gazed out at the miles of gardens stretching as far as the eye could see. The ranch was the largest in the Valley with the Dillons' Saguaro Winery a close second.

An orographic effect of cloud formation and with it lots of moisture had created this lush, verdant valley surrounded by mountains with desert on the far sides to the east, west, north, and south. A handful of enormous ranches, including Morgan's Run and the Dillons', and a few smaller ones made up much of the largely undeveloped Saguaro Valley. Three thousand year-round residents and an equal number of snowbirds, tourists, and wealthy vacationers enjoyed its beauty and abundance. Over the years, the Valley's wealthiest residents had bought up the land, then deeded it back to conservancy groups with the understanding that they could farm it, but that it could never be developed.

"Paradise," she sighed, leaning back. "Don't know how you ever left."

"Sedona's none too shabby even though it's been overrun by touristas. Course, if that wasn't the case, I'd be out of a job. I guess you could say I'm a part of its demise."

"It's still gorgeous. I went camping there with friends a few years ago."

Not as gorgeous as you. "You should come up again sometime. I could show you the sights."

She turned to him, his beautiful smile melting her heart as her inner voice cried, *Stay away! Do not get involved.* "Maybe."

"Can I ask you something?"

"Of course."

"Did I hurt your feelings after Beth's wedding? I mean, we had a good time. Were you wanting more when I hightailed it back to Sedona?"

She shrugged, gazing toward the mountains. "It was a wedding. Everyone has a good time at weddings. Then we all go back to real life." *What a load of horseshit!*

Surprised at her change in tone, he stared at her. "I'm sorry if I misunderstood. Just seems like most of the time we're together, you look like you'd rather be a million miles away."

"It's been a rough year."

He reached over and attempted to take her hand.

Hope stood, throwing her half-full beer in the trash. "I've got to get going. Beth needs me to bring some things to the hospital."

Robbie watched her practically running to her truck. "See you tomorrow?"

"Absolutely," she called back to him, waving over her shoulder. *I must look like a first-class idiot!*

CHAPTER 22

When Hope arrived at the hospital, Beth and Lang were just finishing dinner, the baby asleep beside them. "Hi, you three. How's it going?"

"Great," Lang said as his wife gave her a wan smile.

Hope smiled at her friend, who looked exhausted, dark circles under her soft brown eyes. "I hope I got everything you need," she said, holding up a small duffle. "Shall I unpack these things?"

"No, come sit," Beth said, patting the bed beside her.

"I tell you what, ladies. I have a few phone calls to make, so I'll leave you two to catch up." He leaned over and kissed Beth's forehead. "Okay?"

She nodded, hand stroking his cheek.

Hope took the chair Lang vacated and pulled it alongside the bed, taking Beth's hand. "Your husband's a sweetheart."

"Yes, he is," Beth said. "He's gonna be a great dad, but it's nice to have a tiny break. I'm not used to so much hovering. I'm kind of a loner, as you know."

"Once you get some rest, things'll look brighter."

"Rest? I understand that I won't be rested again for at least two years. What was I thinking? I need a lot of sleep!"

Hope glimpsed the panic in her friend's eyes. "That's why I'm here."

"But you'll be leaving and I have the farm to run and oh, my God, Hope, I love Lily and Lang. They're my whole world, but I don't think I can do this!"

"Hey, relax. I've never been in your shoes," she said. *And I never will be.* A lump formed in her throat. "But I hear that postpartum depression can be ferocious."

Beth watched her friend's eyes fill with tears, and she reached out. "Oh, Hope, I'm sorry to be complaining after everything you've gone through. What a selfish bitch I must sound like."

Drying her eyes with a coarse hospital tissue, Hope smiled. "You don't sound like a selfish bitch. You sound like a very tired new mom. Do you want to sleep? Shall I go?"

"No, please don't go. Tell me about the farm. You've been up there, haven't you?"

Hope recounted the highlights of the past two days as Beth nodded sleepily. When she finished, she said, "You really want to take a nap, don't you?"

"Not until you tell me about my brother."

"Which one?"

"You know who I mean. Has he made a pass at you?"

Hope's face reddened as she looked up at Beth with startled eyes. "That obvious, huh? I've gotta get a better poker face."

"He's a flirt, just like the rest of my siblings, including Ruthie, but he's interested, Hopie. More than I've seen him with any other woman."

"Is that meant to be encouraging?"

Beth laughed. "No, my brothers are shameless lotharios. Ignore his flirting. Play hard to get."

She shrugged, blushing again. "We're going out to dinner tomorrow night."

"Oh, dear."

"Strictly business!"

"Good! Trouble is, you like him, don't you?"

Hope nodded. "But I can't get involved. Too soon."

"Then don't. Robbie's a big boy. He'll understand. Besides, he's a great dancer, much better than the others."

"Don't I know it. That's how I originally fell under his charms, as you well remember."

"Be strong. Just stay friends. Doesn't mean you can't still have fun at the next wedding, right?"

"Right!" Hope smiled as the baby stirred.

Beth reached over and picked up the tiny bundle. "Come on, Lil, let's give it another try." She opened her nightgown's front and brought the baby to breast. "My sister's off, I hear."

"So I understand."

"Craziness," Beth said as she maneuvered the now fussy infant around, offering Lily her breast. "My parents are ready to kill her. Oh, Lily, please, what am I doing wrong?" Tears sprang to Beth's eyes as she continued to struggle.

"Want me to get the nurse?"

"No…yes…I don't know! This has been going on for two days and nights! One of the nurses is a lactation specialist. She's been in many times. They've had to give Lily formula 'cause I can't feed her." Tears streamed down her cheeks and Beth's thin shoulders trembled. "I can't do it, Hope. I just can't!"

"Let me see if I can find the nurse," Hope said, rising and stepping out.

She returned immediately with a nurse. "Okay, hon, let's see what we can do."

Leonora followed in their wake, ready to jump in.

"Hey, Beth, I'll let these pros take over," Hope said, bending over to hug and kiss her friend. "I'll see you soon, and please call if you need anything, okay?"

Beth nodded, as her mother and the nurse, swooped in.

CHAPTER 23

"Hey, son," Ben Senior called from the front porch as Robbie hopped out of his truck. "Come have a cold one with your old man."

"Hey, Dad, I'll grab something and be right out."

A few minutes later, beer in hand, he sat in a rocker next to his father and leaned back. "Love this view of the ranch."

His dad smiled. "Me, too. 'Sides, afternoon sun is too bright on the terrace."

"Sure is nice at sunset, though."

"You bet. How's things up at the farm?"

"Busy. Beth and Raoul have a well-oiled machine up there. I don't think a couple of greenhorns will muck it up too badly."

His father noticed he did not mention Ruthie. *When will my baby find her place?* "How's Hope doin'? Not exactly her line of work."

"She's great. Incredibly strong and a hard worker. She's been picking and I've been with Raoul and the guys. I suspect Beth's been doin' some of the office work in the hospital."

His father chuckled. "I expect she is. Poor baby's having a rough start. Needs to rest, but you know Bethie."

"Definitely the most driven one of us. How'd that happen?"

"Your sister's a listener. She listens, then does. No fanfare. By the way, Lang stopped in. He says Hope's been a huge help to them. Nice girl, Hope."

Robbie gazed over at his father, who was about as subtle as a sledgehammer. "Yeah, she's great."

"Glad she's on the ranch for a while. Had a tough year, poor thing."

"Yeah, everyone keeps saying she's had a bad year. What happened?"

"Lost someone close to her, an old friend, I understand. I suspect there's more to the story, but not sure what. Your mom tried like heck to wheedle it outta Beth, but I don't believe she was successful."

Robbie gazed out at the flower gardens covering his parents' front yard and beyond the yard to the distant mountains. *Stay out of this, Morgan. It's not your business.*

"You like her, don't you?" his dad asked.

"Who, Hope?"

His father grinned, raising an eyebrow.

"She's great, Dad, but I'm leavin' soon and I'm not the best relationship material."

"Maybe you just haven't found the right gal."

"Dad, if Hope's had a rough year, I'm the last person she needs to get involved with."

Ben Senior shrugged. "Sellin' yerself short as usual, son."

"And what's that supposed to mean?"

"You and Ruthie are my dreamers."

"Please don't lump me together with Ms. Flibbertigibbet!"

His father chuckled. "It's a good thing, dreamin'. Just meant you haven't found yourselves yet. Sometimes it seems to this old man like you don't think you deserve to."

"Cause I haven't seen the light and come back home?"

Ben Senior smiled at his son, the spitting image of the woman he had loved for over forty years. "No secret that I'd love all my children to be living here at the ranch. We miss you when you're not here, but I wasn't talkin' about that. I was talking about what's really important—your happiness. Findin' the right partner trumps geography any day, son."

"Well, Ruthie's all set. She's found Kevin."

"If you believe that, I've got some snake oil to sell ya."

Robbie grinned. "What, you don't think Kevin's in it for the long haul?"

"Don't know what Langdon's thinkin', but someday he'll get his head out of his you-know-where."

"You think they're destined to be together?"

"Yup, but she's young yet and I think Harley knows that and is biding his time. Anyway, we were talkin' about you."

"Hopeless, Dad," he said as the Volvo came down the drive and Kyle and his mother hopped out.

Chapter 24

Robbie made a reservation at the Red Mesa Inn, and caught Hope Tuesday afternoon as she was heading out.

She paused at her truck. "That sounds great. I've heard of it, but never been there. It's kind of fancy, though, isn't it?" *And the top romantic spot in the Southwest.*

"Runs the gamut, I think. Maybe not these muddy jeans," he said, gesturing at his clothes, a layer of dirt covering every inch of him, including his face. "But I don't think it's too fancy. I'll probably just clean up, but no jacket and tie, I hope. I'll ask the folks and call if we need formal duds."

She laughed. "Thanks. Still six?"

"You bet." He tipped his hat, thinking how lovely she looked, the afternoon catching flecks of gold in the strands of hair that fell across her eyes. *You'd look sexy as hell in a burlap bag,* he mused, watching as she hopped into the truck and gave him a shy wave.

Beth and Lang had just arrived home when Hope drove in. She helped them take the last of the baby's things from the car. As she followed them in, she felt a pang of guilt. "Lang, I didn't think. Do you need help tonight? I can call Robbie and reschedule."

"No way, Jose. We'll be fine. Give us a chance to settle in. Also give you a night out before you're on duty."

"Of course. You'd like time alone."

"He's kidding about the duty part, too," Beth said. "He's staying home tomorrow. Thursday Ruthie'll be back at the farm, so they'll be fine if you're here with me."

Lily in her arms, Beth followed her husband into the kitchen, where he began unpacking food and supplies from their stop at the grocery store. Hope watched as he stacked a few cans of formula on the counter, then turned to Beth, who had settled in a chair with the sleeping baby.

Beth's eyes filled with tears. "Nursing's not going well. They sent us home with a pump and I'm gonna keep trying, but they told me I have to keep supplementing with the formula."

"Oh, sweetie, you never know. When you get some rest, your milk may come in."

"That's what Maggie said, but I'm not hopeful."

"Speaking of rest," he said, "why don't you and Lily head upstairs and I'll bring you some dinner in a little while. God knows we've got enough to feed an army. What'll it be?"

"Just some soup, and maybe toast," she said. "But I can fix it later."

"Come on," Hope said, extending her hand. "Let him pamper you while it lasts. You can help me choose my ensemble for tonight."

Beth smiled and took her hand. "Okay, okay, I surrender."

Hope settled Beth and the baby, then took a shower. After scouring her closet, she brought a few items in to ask her friend's advice. "I like the blue skirt and that lacy top."

"I have a few pairs of dressy slacks, but I left most of my dresses at home. In fact, I have no idea what I'll wear to the wedding. Dumb planning. I can run down next week."

"Or visit Gabriela's. You won't recognize yourself when she gets through with you. Her clothes are amazing and she's like a fairy godmother. One or two waves of her wand and *poof*—you're Cinderella."

"I hope not!"

"Watch Lily for a sec," Beth said, hopping up from the bed. She returned with several dresses, one of which caught Hope's eye immediately.

"Yes, I agree," Beth said, following her gaze. "You'll look spectacular in this. Try it on."

Hope threw off her robe and slipped into the pale rose sheath with a beaded top. It fit perfectly, hugging her thin body in all the right places. "Too bad it's a bit too tight."

"Is not!" Beth cried. "Fits you a hell of a lot better than me. You'll have my brother drooling the moment he catches sight of you. I have a shawl that looks sensational with it. Have you got shoes?"

Hope retrieved beige heels from her closet and returned to find her friend holding a soft cream-colored shawl and delicate silver necklace.

"I've got earrings, too!" Beth said. Lily stirred as Beth rifled through her jewelry box, producing several pairs of earrings. "You choose."

"Thanks, dearie, but I've got earrings that will look great with this necklace. You take care of your sweetie pie and I'll pull myself together."

She disappeared into her room to dab on a little makeup and lipstick. She then found the earrings she sought, a gift from Bruce several months before he died. She felt the familiar ache and sighed. *I wonder if tonight is a good idea?*

Shaking herself, Hope returned to find Beth changing the baby. She looked up and smiled. "Wow! You'll knock his socks off! Remember, play hard to get."

Hope laughed. "There won't be any getting. I'm still on the bench." *But anticipating tonight has sure been a lot of fun, and I haven't even laid eyes on Mr. Sexy!*

Robbie was waiting in the living room, talking with Lang. Hope's mouth dropped open when she spied him. *Mr. Sexy didn't even come close!* He wore black dress jeans and boots, a gray sport coat, and a blue oxford shirt that turned his green eyes azure. *Oh, my, does he clean up well!*

"Hi," she sputtered.

"Hi, yourself. You look sensational." *Who are you kidding, buddy? If she looked any better, I'd drop to my knees and propose.* No woman had ever had this effect on Robbie, and he wasn't sure how to handle it.

Lang watched the interplay between them, a wide grin on his face. "Have a good time, you two. We'll leave the light on, Hope."

"Thanks, but I won't be late."

That's what you think, Lang mused. *If Robbie Morgan doesn't cool his jets, you may never come back.* "Buddy, take care of our nanny."

"Will do," Robbie said, opening the door for Hope. As she passed by, her familiar scent of sandalwood and orange surrounded him.

Quiet on the drive, as they neared the Red Mesa he said, "Thanks for coming tonight."

"My pleasure. It's good to get out." She glanced over to find him smiling. As a consequence, she didn't see a truck pulling out of the restaurant lot until they were almost upon it. "Robbie, watch out!" she cried as he swerved just in time.

A few minutes later, safely parked, he came round and opened her door. "Sorry about that. Honestly, I couldn't take my eyes off you. Not wise when driving." His words, while true, were intended to lighten the mood, but instead, he watched her stiffen. "Hope, I'm sorry. Didn't mean to spook you."

"It's fine," she said, turning to him. "Just a little shaken up."

"Shall we?" he asked, lightly taking her arm.

His touch warmed her in ways she didn't want to think about. *It's alright, girl. You can do this. A casual date with a handsome guy. You deserve it. Just don't put too much into it. Casual, casual, casual!*

Chapter 25

"So, do you love Sedona?" she asked, sipping the wine he'd ordered, an excellent red from the Dillons' Saguaro Winery. They sat in a shady spot on the restaurant's western-facing veranda. Heaters lined the porch, providing warmth against the evening chill.

Robbie shrugged. "It's been good. I work with a great crew. We're all friends. Our boss can be a jerk, but most of the time he's away at one of his five homes all over the world."

"Adventure touring must be lucrative," she said, smiling. She thought back to his touch on her back and shivered.

"You cold? I can ask for an inside table."

"No, this is lovely."

"My jacket?"

She laughed. "I'm fine, really! Now, about your boss?"

"He's got a million irons in the fire. I suspect he makes more on all the properties he owns than the touring business. He has holdings everywhere." He met her eyes and felt himself harden, a rush of feeling sweeping over him. *What is it about her?*

"So, you'll stay up there for a while?"

"Most likely. I'd like to go out on my own. A couple of us have been talking about it. Maybe someday. Truth is, I'd rather be here, even though I'd never tell my parents that, and don't you repeat it."

"My lips are sealed." *Although they'd rather be sealed with yours.* "Would you do the same kind of thing here?"

"Not if it'd wreck the Valley."

"Don't your dad and his buddies own most of the land? They'd never let that happen."

"Maybe. Developers can be relentless though. But never mind about me. What about you? You gonna stay in Tintown?"

"That's where my shop and studio are."

"Beth tells me you've had a rough year. I'm sorry about your friend. Were you close?"

Hope's face paled and her eyes filled with tears. "Very."

"Hope, I'm sorry. I didn't mean to be nosy."

"It's okay," she said, dabbing her eyes with the corner of her napkin.

As Jacob, their waiter, approached, he leaned forward. "You want a few minutes before we order?"

She shook her head. "You go first. I'll decide while you order."

Robbie ordered one of the specials, the Valley mixed grill, the pork and beef from Morgan's Run.

"Excellent choice, sir," Jacob said, turning to her. "And for you, madam?"

"I'll have the trout special," she said. "Do you think I should have ordered a white wine?"

"It's your choice, but I think you'll find the Saguaro Pinot a perfect complement," Jacob said.

"Perfect. Then I'll stick with it," she said.

Jacob took their menus, nodded, and disappeared.

"Hope, I apologize again, no more personal questions. Tell me about your work."

She swallowed hard. "His name was Bruce Cobb. We grew up together. He went away to college and we lost touch for a long period. We had occasional flings when we did get together, which were never the best idea."

"That's tough, to lose someone you've known for so long."

"After college at UCLA, he came home and joined the Border Patrol. He was dark-skinned and spoke fluent Spanish, so he was sent to Mexico undercover. He was far from home last year, working just outside of Juarez when he was killed. A farmer found his body. He'd been tortured, probably for several days." Her voice was a whisper now and tears streamed down her face.

"Oh, God, Hope, I am so sorry." He stood and came to her side, kneeling and placing his arms around her, relieved that they were a distance far from the adjoining tables.

"Me, too." She placed her head on his shoulder as her body trembled with sobs.

After what seemed like hours, she settled and raised her head. "Thanks. I'm okay. I needed to do that. It's been a rough few months and I rarely let myself cry."

"It's very cathartic, I hear," he said, standing and offering her a starched white handkerchief.

"Thanks," she said, a slight smile playing round her eyes. "Do handsome cowboys always have a handkerchief in a crisis?"

He laughed. "Don't know about the handsome part, but I always have one in my pocket. Trail dust. Kicks up my allergies big time. Usually have a bandana, but since we were coming here, I figured that one would do. Found it in my drawer."

"It will do just fine," she said. "Now please sit and enjoy your wine."

Over fresh jicama salads, they talked about her work and life in Tintown, and by the time Jacob arrived with their entrees, the mood had lightened. "Can I get you anything else, folks?"

"Thanks, we're good," Robbie said, nodding to the slim, dark-haired waiter.

Hope watched him, marveling as she always did at the Morgan charm. *Stops everyone in their tracks, male or female.*

After an incredible meal, they declined dessert, but ordered espressos, which they took to a small garden just down and to the right of the veranda steps. "This sure is a beautiful spot," she said, sitting on a wrought iron loves seat, flower beds with winter blooms surrounding them.

"That it is. Apparently there's a walled garden somewhere."

"Yes, Beth told me about it. Lang and she have eaten there several times."

"Very romantic, I understand."

"So I hear."

"Maybe someday we can try it?" he asked, reaching to take her hand. "When you're ready. When *we're* ready?"

Hope squeezed his hand. "Maybe," she said, taking a sip of her coffee as she gazed at the beauty all around them. Resisting the urge to fling herself into his arms, she stayed still and silent, enjoying the cool breeze of the evening and the scent of jasmine in the air.

Finally he turned to her. "What d'ya think? Should I go settle up with Jacob?"

CHAPTER 26

As they neared the ranch, he pulled over and parked. "I don't want this night to end yet."

Surprised, she gazed over at him. "Me, either."

Before she knew it, Robbie drew her close, lips on hers, a deep lingering kiss to which she responded, her tongue finding his, delving, stroking, teasing. Hope felt his strong chest against her breasts and opened herself as his fingers teased and stroked her nipples through the dress's thin fabric. As she reached up to caress his cheek and neck and run her fingers through his hair, headlights crested the hill and a truck approached.

Breathless, they pulled apart as the truck's driver braked and stopped. Harley Langdon rolled down the window. "Hey, folks, everything okay?" he asked, a wide grin on his face. "You broken down?"

"Fine, Harl," Robbie said, his face beet red. "What're you doin' out here so late?"

"On my way north to see Willow, but I realized I left my wallet at the stables."

"How long you gone for?" Robbie asked, making small talk.

"Day after Christmas. Well, I'll let you two get on with things," he said, a wolfish grin playing across his face.

"Yeah, right," Robbie said. "Have a great holiday and say hi to Willow for me."

With a wave, Harley said, "Don't do anything I wouldn't do!"

Hope groaned, hands over her face. "We'll be the talk of the town."

He laughed. "I doubt it. Harley may be a lot of things, but he's discreet. He might tell Ben cause those guys have no secrets, but that's as far as it'll go."

"What about Maggie?"

"She's discreet, too. Beth and Lang know we went out. It'll be okay." He drew her close.

"Oh, no you don't, not here!" she said, as every inch of her body screamed with desire.

"Well, let's see. There's the big house, but I think my folks are home."

"Don't be ridiculous. Home or not, I'm not having your mom and dad find us in your bed. Probably still has its Cowboy Bob sheets."

"Hey, how'd you know?"

"Lucky guess," she said. He was grinning, desire and lust shining in his gorgeous, moonlit eyes. "Time for you to take me home."

"Hold on, hold on," he said, hand stroking her thigh. "I'm getting signals that you're not opposed to us continuing this if we could find a good venue, right?"

Robbie Morgan, you are a wolf! Hope nodded, chiding her weakness. She wanted him so badly it hurt.

"I've got an idea. Hold that feeling!"

He drove past the big house and stables, then circled round, taking the hill road to the Lodge. He parked in the far lot nearest the Spa and came round to open her door. "Come on!"

"Where are you taking me?" she asked, accepting his hand.

"You'll see," he whispered, guiding her round to the back entrance. On most nights, the Spa closed at nine, so the building was dark. He used his key to get in and led her down a hall lined with closed doors on either side. Midway along, he stopped and opened one of the doors. "Here we are, my lady," he said, flicking on a light. "Oh, too bright." He turned back and slid the switch dimming the overhead light. It was a massage room, tidy, and clinical, the bed neatly laid out for the first client in the morning.

Without waiting for her to speak, he drew her close and kissed her deeply, his lips then moving to her neck and shoulders. Hope had never wanted anyone more in her life, but she pulled away, breathless. "No, Robbie, this is crazy. I can't, not now, not here."

"Is it the room or me?"

"Both…neither…I don't know. I'm sorry."

"Moment gone?"

"Yes, I'm sorry."

His hand cupped her chin gently. "Hey, I understand. I get it. No need to apologize. But we had a moment, right?"

She nodded.

"Then if we had a moment, that means it's possible, and we might have one again when things feel right?"

Hope nodded again as he leaned forward and kissed her forehead. "Come on, sweetie, let's get you home."

He turned away and she touched his arm. When he looked back, she said, "Thank you, Robbie."

"For what? Trying to seduce you in the massage room?"

Hope laughed. "No, for understanding."

"No problem. Come on."

When he stopped the car in front of Beth and Lang's, he turned to her. "Okay if I walk you to the door?"

"Of course."

She opened the door. No sign of Lang or Beth. "Wanta come in?"

"Better not. Don't want to wake Lily or her parents."

"Okay, well…night. I had a really good time."

"Me, too. Can I kiss you?"

In answer, she folded her arms round his neck and drew him to her, initiating what turned into a long, lingering kiss that almost brought both of them to their knees.

"The massage room is looking pretty good right now," he said, breathless, as she turned to go in.

"Yes, it is," she said, smiling as she stepped over the threshold. "Good night."

Chapter 27

Robbie arrived at the farm at six a.m. and worked nonstop until after five. Hope was home assisting with the baby, so he had spent the day running back and forth from the animals to the gardens. Mostly he had been in the gardens, harvesting and processing fruits, vegetables, and herbs. Morgan's Run herbs, especially their lavender, were sought after worldwide. Not only did herbalists and essential oil producers regularly order the farm's bounty, but several natural grocers stocked Morgan's Run herbs. Companies often angled to have exclusive rights to the herbs, but Beth and Ruth refused. They appreciated the wider distribution and also saw the oils as another growth opportunity for future.

At the end of the day, Robbie sat on the farm porch, watching sheep graze in a far meadow, three Australian shepherds keeping them from straying far from the flock. All day he had looked over his shoulder, wondering if Hope might come up for a few hours. Truth was, he missed her. He decided he'd clean up and pay a visit to his newest niece before dinner.

*****

Beth and Hope sat on the terrace, watching the sunset, the baby sleeping on her mother's chest.

"I'm going to give it a few more days. Then I'm going to take the pump back and accept failure," Beth said, gazing toward the mountains.

"You're not a failure. So many women struggle with breastfeeding."

"Not earth mothers like Maggie who provide all their babies' nourishment for their first year."

"I think she said six months," Hope said, stroking her friend's arm. "And you're queen of the earth mothers, so don't beat yourself up."

"I'm not sure I'm cut out for this, Hope. I love Lily, but this is not who I am, you know?"

"Give yourself time, sweetie. This is postpartum fatigue talking."

"I know, I know. I'm hoping Haley will help me get through this." She referred to her therapist, Haley Alvarez, who had come to her wedding and was now a dear friend.

"You love her, don't you?"

"She saved my life after Bill. How are he and our fellow climbers, by the way? Have you seen much of them?"

"I haven't been hiking much this past year. Too many things going on. When I do go, I try to avoid Bill the pill."

"Don't dislike him on my account."

"I don't, but his breaking your heart did not endear me to him."

"Me, neither," Beth said, smiling. "But remember, if we hadn't broken up, I'd never have gotten together with Lang."

"That's very true. You're so lucky. I've never seen two people so in love, except perhaps your older brother and Maggie."

"Ben and Mags have had their ups and downs."

"So do you think Haley would see me?"

"Absolutely."

"I mean, since I'm your friend. Sometimes therapists don't like to see friends."

"That's only if the friend is the issue you're struggling with. I hope that's not true?"

Hope laughed. "Definitely not, but what about the friend's brother?"

"Call Haley. See what she says. She's seen my brothers in action and knows them pretty well, although not Robbie so much."

"I'll think about it. Can I get you anything? A sweater?"

"No, the dinner was incredible and little Lil here is keeping me plenty warm."

"Thank your mother-in-law's chef for dinner. He's a great guy, by the way."

"Jon? Yes, he is. Martha's always worried that he'll want to return to California, but I think he's pretty well settled in the fabulous apartment she decorated for him."

"Has she got another? I could get used to Valley living."

"Oh, Hope, we'd love it if you'd come to live in Saguaro!"

"Pipe dream," she said, smiling at her friend. "I'm pretty settled in Tintown."

"If you have to live in Tucson, that's sure a cool area."

"Hey, hon, I'm back!" Lang called from the kitchen door. "You ladies need anything out there?"

"Thanks, we're fine," Beth said. "How were your parents?"

Lang strolled up and kissed the top of Beth's head. "Mom's fine. Says she's coming up to help out tomorrow morning. Did she run that by you?"

"Yes."

"Well, I told her to keep it short."

"Lang, you did not! It's fine. Besides, it will give Hope a break so she can paint."

"Mom's a hoverer. Gotta nip that in the bud or she'll be living here. Anything to get away from Dad. Want me to take Lily?"

"Let sleeping puppies lie," Beth said, patting the baby. "Is someone here? I thought I heard a car."

Lang walked to the side of the terrace where the driveway was visible. "Looks like Uncle Robbie's truck. I wonder why he's here?" he added, grinning at Hope.

"He's here to see his niece, of course," Hope said, aware that her cheeks were bright red.

"And escape from Mom," Beth said, waving as her brother stepped out the back door.

"Hey, Rob!"

"Hey, buddy," Lang said. "Want a beer?"

"Thanks, I'm good." He glanced at Hope, noticing her bright red cheeks, then turned to his sister and baby. "How's my niece?"

"Doin' fine," Beth said as he stooped and kissed her cheek, then the baby's.

"Can I hold her?"

Beth hesitated, not wanting to wake the infant, but then handed her to her brother.

Robbie cradled her gently in his arms, gazing down at the tiny bundle wrapped in pale green swaddling. "Looks like a little green pickle," he said, eyes full of love.

Hope watched him, amazed at his gentleness, the same gentleness he'd shown with her, even in the heat of passion. *What a wonderful father he'll make.*

"So, how was everything up there today?" Beth asked.

"Hoppin'."

As brother and sister talked about the farm, the others listened quietly. Hope marveled as she always did at the siblings' affection and closeness. Beth might have been the quiet one who kept herself apart from the fray, but she was certainly well loved by all members of the amazing Morgan family.

Finally Lily began to fuss. Robbie said, "Sis, 'fraid I can't give her what she probably wants right now," he said, smiling at her.

"Neither can I, apparently," Beth said, standing up and taking the baby. "Honey, will you come in with me and help with bottle warming? I'll try, but I doubt I'll succeed."

When the parents departed, leaving them alone, Robbie turned to Hope. "Busy day, huh?"

"Not as busy as yours."

"Wanta take a walk? There's a wide-open trail behind the barn. Easy to follow on a night like this."

"Okay. Let me grab a sweater."

Hope stepped inside and grabbed a sweater from the hook by the door. "We're taking a walk." As usual, the nursing was not going well and her friend looked frustrated and distraught. "Unless you need me?"

"No, dearie, same ole same ole. Have fun and take your time. I'm about to cry uncle and let Lang feed her the bottle so I can take a shower."

"You sure?"

"Absolutely. Now, shoo!"

CHAPTER 28

"Beautiful," he said as Hope rejoined him on the terrace. *And I'm not talking about this clear, starry night.* She had pulled on a worn, light blue sweater. Even in the darkness, the moonlight lit up her eyes.

"Seems like nights like this are the norm around here," she said, trying to ignore the intensity in his gaze.

"Except during the rainy seasons. We get much more rain than Tucson."

She nodded. "Hence the fertile valley."

He led her down the lawn. "This way."

"Haven't tried that trail yet. Are you sure it's safe?"

He held out one hand and waved a flashlight with the other. "And what do I do for a living?"

Laughing, Hope took his hand, warmth coursing through her. "Lead on, oh expert guide," she said. *And let's hope my quivery legs don't give out on me!*

The full moon illuminated the way, the flashlight unnecessary. Ordinarily Hope would have been terrified of snakes and other creatures, but she felt safe beside him as they climbed the hill behind the house. The trail turned east and followed the ridge for a time. They chatted about this and that, their work, the baby, and the ups and downs of the Morgan family.

"I've said it before and I'll say it again. You are so lucky to have your family."

"Yeah, they're pretty great. Tell me about yours. Your mom? Your brothers?"

"Tom's the oldest. He's married, two kids. He and Betsy are pretty happy, stable people. He runs a seed store in Prescott and Betsy teaches first grade. Bart's another story. Pretty much a fuck-up, excuse my language. In and out of rehab for drugs and alcohol since he was fifteen. Mom's tried everything to get him help, but he always lapses. When he's sober, he visits once in a while, mostly begging for money. I haven't seen him since Bruce's funeral. He came stoned out of his mind and we haven't spoken since."

"Must be tough."

She shrugged. "Our family's been screwed up my entire life, long before my dad walked out, which is why I envy you and yours so much. When Beth first brought me here, I was amazed. I never knew families like this existed in real life."

"We have our moments, believe me. What about your mom?"

"She's in Tintown. On her third husband, Ralph, who is actually a great guy. Can't believe she found him. Her second husband, Perry, was a nightmare. Ralph's been great to her and me. He's also tried to help Bart, but that's a lost cause at the moment."

"Here we are," he said, leading her to an open spot where soft grass formed a circle surrounded by rock and scrub brush.

"What's this?"

"It's called Jake's Pillow. Jay Dillon claims his father created it years ago as a sacred place where he could come to be alone. Never knew him, but all reports say he was a son of a bitch."

"Yet he created this beautiful place? Who keeps it up?"

"That's the mystery. Apparently no one, although everyone suspects that one of Jaybo Dillon's men comes out regularly and mows and trims it."

"A mysterious place, in the middle of paradise. How fitting!" Hope twirled around, taking in the craggy boulders and tall brush and trees.

"Yes, how fitting," he said, taking her hand and attempting to draw her close.

"And convenient. Did you have this in mind when you suggested a walk?" she asked, standing her ground.

"Does it matter?"

"No, I guess not…but…on second thought, yes, it does. Don't you think we should have talked about this? I'm still not sure this is a great idea."

"Then let's head back," he said, eyes soft as he gazed at her. "If that's what you want?"

"I don't know what I want."

"Then let's not push things until you do."

"I'm sorry."

"Hope, there's nothing to apologize for. You've been through hell this year and you're with a cowboy who's at loose ends with no plans for the future. A cowboy who, I might add, didn't treat you all that well at our first acquaintance."

"What do you mean? You treated me great. I just put too much into it. That's all."

"Wanta sit down and watch the moon, no funny business?"

She laughed. "Funny business?"

"You know what I mean. We can just sit and talk."

"What if I don't want to sit and talk?"

"Then we'll head back."

"What if I don't want to head back, cowboy?" she asked, moving closer to him, arms circling his neck.

CHAPTER 29

Robbie felt his erection grow as her touch ignited every inch of his body. "Is this what's called a change of heart?" he asked, voice husky. Gently he embraced her, his hand stroking her thin, graceful back.

She smiled. "I believe it is. Could be the best or worst idea I've ever had. Want to help me find out which?"

"Whatever you say, cowgirl."

"Cowgirl?"

"How's beautiful?"

"Better," she said, her lips finding his. Their kiss was deep, full of their mutual longing.

"Oh, God, Hope, are you sure?"

"Yes," she whispered, nibbling his ear.

"Cause I'm not sure I can stop this time."

"I won't let you," she said. Her hand reached down to stroke him. Stunned by the size of him, she gasped.

"May I?" he whispered, hands holding the hem of her sweater. She nodded and Robbie pulled it and tee shirt over her head, leaving only her bra.

"Beautiful," he said, leaning to kiss her soft, round breasts encased in lace.

As Hope sighed, his hands unhooked the back and the bra fell to the ground. "You warm enough, love?"

She nodded.

"Good," he said, taking one breast into his mouth, his tongue circling and teasing the nipple to hardness.

"Oh, oh," she cried as he moved to the other breast.

"Let me love you, Hope. I promise I won't hurt you, okay?"

"Yes, please," she said as her hands moved to divest him of his shirt, which he hastily laid on the ground.

Before she knew what was happening, he had unzipped her jeans and slid them downward. "Okay, cowboy. You, too," she said, surprised at her boldness. With that, she unzipped his fly, releasing him. As her hands wrapped around him, Hope gasped.

"Don't be scared, sweetheart. I'll go slow. By the time I'm finished, you'll be ready for me."

"Oh, Robbie, I…I…"

"I know, love. Come on," he said, gently bringing her to lie on the ground, their clothes under her.

After a deep, lingering kiss, his lips, hands, and fingers began a slow, sensuous descent from her neck to her quivering breasts. She caressed him with her fingers, marveling at his strong, muscular chest and abdomen. "Let me, Hope. Please let me," he said, as he guided her hands back around his neck. Hope sighed as he parted her legs and his fingers delved into her sweet wetness.

"Oh, Robbie, please," she begged, drawing him closer. "I need you inside me."

"Not yet, my love," he said huskily, fighting hard to maintain control.

His lips and tongue replaced fingers and teased and probed until Hope thought she'd go crazy with longing. "Oh, oh, oh!" she cried as a crashing climax overtook her.

As the crescendos subsided, Robbie pushed up on his elbows, gazing down at her. "You ready?"

She nodded and he reached for his jeans. "Not necessary," she whispered, and he gazed back in amazement.

"You have birth control?"

Breathless, she said, "Yes. Please don't make me wait any longer."

With that, he leaned down, kissing her deeply, tongue circling hers as she responded in kind. "You are one amazing woman, Hope Seymour," he said as he raised his hips, his penis tickling between her open legs, her soft depths waiting for him. Gently and slowly he entered her, tentative at first, teasing and stroking her as he deepened each thrust.

"Please, Robbie!" she cried, pulling him down. "I need all of you."

"Me, too, baby," he said as he went all the way, filling her as Hope would never have imagined possible.

Complete, she sighed, her last coherent thought as they moved together in a riotous, passionate ecstasy that seemed to last forever.

"Oh, my sweet, sweet, baby," he whispered in her ear as they reached a crashing, simultaneous climax.

Afterward, as they lay entwined, Hope felt love, *his love* as it filled her, keeping her warm, safe, and complete. "Thank you," she whispered, kissing his shoulder.

"No, my sweetheart, thank you, for giving yourself to me."

As he kissed her softly, Hope felt him harden inside her, and their amazing dance began again, this time more slowly, less frantic, every thrust filling her more completely. She couldn't get enough of him as she lifted her hips to invite him deeper.

"Oh, my love, my love," he murmured, "not sure how long I can hang on, but you are perfect."

"Hmm, I doubt that," she said, kissing his strong neck, inviting him deeper and deeper with every thrust, legs wrapped around him as she arched her slender back.

Later, as they lay still and sated, she shivered, the night air now cool. "Hey, you're cold," he said huskily. "We'd better go."

"No, not yet. Just a few more minutes, okay?" she said, squeezing and holding him inside her, refusing to let go.

"I'd happily stay like this forever, sweetheart, but it's getting pretty nippy." He captured her lips for a deep, lingering kiss, then moved down her neck to her breasts, finding the nipples rock-hard. "Yup, it's official. You're freezing."

With a groan, he withdrew, and Hope sighed as if one of her vital organs had been ripped out.

Robbie gathered their clothes and dressed her. Hope felt like a limp rag doll in his swift but gentle hands. Finally satisfied that she was set, he turned and threw on his own clothes. She watched, realizing that it was too late. *I'm hopelessly in love with Robbie Morgan and there's not a damn thing I can do about it.*

He gazed over, noticing her expression. "Hey, you okay? You look like you've seen a ghost."

"Something like that," she said, afraid to tell him how she really felt. Clouds now obscured the moon and the temperature had dropped. "You sure you can find our way home?"

He laughed, bending to kiss her sweetly. "As I said earlier, you forget what I do for a living. Come on." He took her hand.

They said good night on Beth and Lang's front porch. "Looks like Lily and parents are in bed."

"Thank goodness. I'm sure I look like a fright."

"You look amazing," he said, kissing her.

Hope felt her knees tremble. "Oh, no, we don't. Good night, cowboy, before you get me into trouble."

"Never. You at the farm tomorrow?"

She shook her head. "I'll be here. Lang's got to be at the office most of the day."

"I'll be in touch," he said, drawing her close. "Tonight was incredible for me."

"Me, too. Night." One squeeze of his hand, and she stepped inside and closed the door, her sigh echoing in the darkened house.

*****

As he drove up his parents' drive, Robbie was surprised to see the house ablaze with lights and his brother Ben's Rover parked alongside his mother's car. He found a solemn group in the living room—both parents, Kyle, and Ben. "Hey, what's up?" he asked, gazing from face to face.

"It's your sister," Leonora said, eyes red-rimmed. "It's always your sister! When will our baby ever grow up?"

"Now, Nora, they're probably fine and decided to stay out another night," Ben Senior said, sounding less than convinced than his words implied.

"What? Ruthie isn't back?" Robbie asked, looking at his brothers.

"Nope," Ben said, shaking his head. "And she's with that bozo who can barely stay seated on his horse."

"Doesn't she have her cell?"

"Probably," his father replied, "but you know how poor service is when you get up in the mountains."

"It's getting cold," Robbie said. "Hope they're hunkered down."

"Oh, dear Lord," his mother wailed. "My poor, poor baby!"

Kyle came to sit beside her, arm circling her shoulders. "Hey, Mom, they'll be fine. Ruthie's a scrapper and she knows the trails. She went off mad and this may be payback."

"Well, if it is, I'll be the first to wallop her," Ben Senior said as all eyes turned to stare at him. Ruthie was his baby and none of them had ever heard him speak a harsh word about her, never mind talk of giving her a wallop!

"What's the plan?" Robbie asked, looking at Ben.

"We'll head out at first light."

"Does Harley know?" Leonora asked.

Ben nodded. "I texted him, but he's with Willow until after the holidays. I encouraged him to stay put until we know more."

"Fat chance of that," a voice said as Harley Langdon stepped into the room.

"Geez, buddy," Ben said. "How'd you get here so fast? You must've gone—"

"Ninety-five, most of the way."

"Harley Langdon, you're crazy!" Leonora said, exchanging looks with her husband.

Crazy in love, Robbie thought, noticing the worry ablaze in the wrangler's intense green eyes. "I'll call my Sedona crew. They can be here by morning to join the search."

"Thanks, son," Ben Senior said, placing a hand on Harley's shoulder. He looked as if he'd aged twenty years.

CHAPTER 30

The Sedona crew, two men and a tall, buxom redhead, arrived at seven a.m. They had a trailer with two all-terrain vehicles and tracking equipment. Robbie greeted them in the drive. The redhead, Jane Mackenzie, made great show of embracing him, provoking sidelong glances from her coworkers. "Hey, handsome, we've missed you!"

"Thanks for coming so quickly," he said, nodding to Dave Burrows and Hal Garrard.

Dave shook his hand. "No, prob, partner. Any word yet?" Freckle-faced, light brown crew cut hair, the short, compact guide was Robbie's age but looked fifteen. An experienced guide, he was dressed for the field in heavy work pants, vest, and green thermal shirt.

"No, but there's basically no cell service beyond the ranch. Come on in. My parents' cook has a huge breakfast laid out."

"Good thing we didn't stop at that diner we passed," Hal said, patting Robbie on the back. The tall, dark-haired man had been Robbie's roommate since their freshman year at college. They still shared an apartment in Sedona, a definite bachelor pad. Garrard was thin, but every inch of him exuded strength, his coal-black eyes watchful and wary. Robbie trusted him with his life and Hal had never let him down. "We'll find her, buddy, he said, "but let's eat first."

His family were well acquainted with Hal, and hugs and handshakes were exchanged all around as Robbie introduced Dave and Jane.

"So great to meet Robbie's family at last!" Jane gushed, throwing herself at his parents and brothers.

The group grabbed plates and had just settled down when Harley walked in with Jeb Barnes.

"Mornin'," Ben Senior said, smiling at the wranglers. "Grab a plate and join us. Jeb, you sure they can spare you at the stables?"

"Nick's got it handled and Maggie'll be there soon."

"Carmela and I will have the children today. Ned's coming over, too," Leonora said.

"What about me, darlin'?" her husband said.

"Oh, pish tush, you, too, of course."

"My future father-in-law is right behind us," Jeb said. "He's watching Toby while Amy's at work."

As if on cue, Spark Foster strolled into the room, Toby in his arms. "Hey, everyone. How can we help?"

"The day care cottage cannot be built fast enough," Leonora said, throwing up her hands. "Have you had breakfast?"

Their old friend nodded. "Hours ago."

"Good. Toby, Emma, and Ben'll be here soon, sweetie. Did someone let Beth and Lang know?"

"I called 'em this morning," Robbie said. "They're on standby, as is Hope."

"Nonsense. She's to stay with Beth," Leonora said. "Now eat up, everyone. Time's a-wastin'."

They all congregated at the stables. The ATVs were useless in the mountains, but Jane, who had little riding experience, planned to take one and circle the town on the wide-open pathways leading out into the foothills. The rest saddled horses and headed out in all directions. "Typical Ruthie," Ben said as he and Kyle rode north. "Didn't bother to tell anyone where the fuck they were headed."

Dave rode south with Jeb. Harley and Hal partnered up and headed west. Robbie planned to join them as soon as he loaded up the ATV and gave Jane directions.

"Rob, hon, I know what I'm doing," she said as she stooped to tie down a flat of water. She wore skin-tight jeans and a V-neck tee shirt. Her utility vest was open, revealing cleavage, which she aimed in his direction.

At that moment, Hope appeared riding Dandy, Jaybo Dillon's chocolate morgan. It was obvious that she had ridden hard. "He's faster than Whimsy and I wanted to keep up," she said, gazing down at his surprised expression.

"What are you doing here, Hope? Beth and Lily need you. We've got plenty of people."

"Martha's there for the day and Lang's working from home in the afternoon," she said, glancing at his redheaded companion.

"This is Jane Mackenzie, one of my Sedona team. She and two others arrived this morning. Jane, this is Hope Seymour."

"Hello," Hope said, smiling, as she patted Dandy. The horse appeared nervous at the sight of the ATV.

"Well, well," Jane said, tipping her baseball cap at the gorgeous blonde, who clearly had something going on with her Robbie. "Nice to meet you. You one of the family, I assume?"

"Friend of the family. Here visiting for a while."

"How nice for you. Rob, hon, I think I'm set. You'd better get going or you'll lose Hal and that gorgeous cowboy."

Robbie waved off the others, who were waiting at the bend in the trail. "Now that Hope's here, we can take the eastern ridge. We'll probably catch sight of you. This way skirts the town for a while."

"Whatever you say, hon. Hopie, we'll see you later." Another tip of her cap and Jane hopped into the ATV.

Robbie untied Royal. "Hold off for a few minutes, Janie. Let us get out of earshot so you don't spook the horses." With that he sprung up on his father's horse and nodded to Hope.

Jane Mackenzie watched them ride out of sight, a frown creasing her brow. *There's something going on with those two and I've gotten here just in time to break it up.* With a roar she started up the ATV and headed toward town.

CHAPTER 31

They rode in silence until they reached Loggerman's Notch, at the crest of a hill about two miles from the stables. The gateway to the eastern mountains and the desert that stretched for miles, the Notch would be the last shade they would enjoy for most of the day. Hope gazed east, wiping dust from her brow. "Wow, what a difference."

"Yup. You get fooled by the Valley and forget that this is what surrounds our little Eden."

"You think they went this way?"

He shrugged, sipping water from his canteen and offering it to her. "Ruthie loves the foothills at the base of the range you see ahead. Whenever she has run away from home, she tends to go this direction, although they could have gone anywhere. The pack trips usually go north. Not much if you head south, but she really likes Mount Lemon, just west of Tucson."

"Needle in a haystack, then?"

"Naw, we'll find 'em. Ben and Harley are great trackers. You gonna be okay? It's gonna be a long day."

She smiled at him. *As long as I'm by your side, I'll be fine.* "Got my panty hose on and plenty of water and snacks. That should keep me going."

"You're amazing. If it weren't for my idiot little sister, I'd find a nice shady spot and ask you to join me."

"No time for funny business. Lead on, cowboy," she said, thinking that the previous night had been anything but funny business!

By prior agreement, all groups turned back in time to reach the stables by sunset. Nick Parker waited to help with the horses, Jane Mackenzie at his side. After tootling around town several times, she had apparently spent the rest of the day tootling around Nick, who looked ready to bolt at the first opportunity.

Ben and Kyle arrived first, then Dave and Jeb. Robbie and Hope had met up with Harley and Hal several hours earlier, and they rode in together.

"Hey, boss," Nick called as Harley and Hal dismounted. "Any sign of 'em?"

Harley shook his head, face grim. "I'm just getting some gear, then heading back out."

"Like hell you are," Ben said.

"Try and stop me," the wrangler said, kicking a wooden bucket as he led his Appaloosa toward the barn. "Hey, Nick, take Pepper in, would you? I've got to make a call."

"Leave him be," Robbie said, grabbing hold of Ben's arm. "He'll cool down."

"Yeah, right," Ben said, shaking loose and following his friend into the barn. Robbie trailed the two men in, and Hope stayed behind to help with the horses.

"How was your ride?" Kyle asked her.

"Hot," she said, smiling. The resemblance between Ben and Kyle was remarkable. Sam, who was due to arrive Saturday, completed the dark-haired, dark-eyed triplets. "And disappointing. I hope they can persuade Harley to wait until it's light."

"You know their history, right? My sister and Harley?"

"I've heard a little."

"She's been in love with him since first grade and he's crazy about her, too. Always claims he holds back 'cause she's too young." Kyle removed his hat, revealing a line of dust across his forehead. He looked tired and as sore as she felt as he led Tara, a sorrel morgan, toward her stall.

When they passed the office, they heard shouting from within. "I can't just sit here!"

"Yes, you can. Poor planning not to bring gear today. That was my fault, but we'll overnight tomorrow, buddy, and as long as we need to until we find them. You know my sister. Always pushing the envelope, always has to go longer and farther. Knowing Ruthie, they most likely went east. We'll find 'em."

"If I get Jack Lighthorse, he can track at night."

"He's away. I already tried him. Now, go home and get some rest. We'll start first thing, at dawn."

"How could she be so stupid?" Harley asked, slumping to sit, head in his hands.

"That'd be Ruthie," Robbie said, patting his shoulder. "But I think she'd call it adventurous."

"Bullshit," Harley said.

"Hey, buddy," Ben said. "Wanta stay with Mags and me tonight?"

Harley rose and shook his head. "Thanks, but I'll head home soon as I check on Pepp. Gotta get packed and clear my head."

Robbie joined Kyle and Hope.

"I'd better head out, too," she said. "Beth and Lang'll be waiting."

"Why don't you leave Dandy here? There are extra stalls and Nick'll take good care of her."

"You bet we will," Jane said, coming up from behind them, leading two of the horses in. "I may not ride, but I know how to take care of these beauties. I'll stay with Nicky till they're all settled."

"Thanks, Janie," Robbie said. "That's a huge help. We'll all be at my parents' when you're done. Nick can drive you up. I'm sure my mother's got rooms all set for you."

"Great. Hope, I'll see you tomorrow morning?"

"Yes, of course," Hope said, eying the other woman's sly grin. *I guess I've been dismissed.*

Robbie watched his coworker disappear into one of the stalls and rolled his eyes. "Ignore that," he whispered.

"Marking her territory?" Kyle asked, grinning from ear to ear. "You didn't tell us there was something going on between you and Janie."

"Because there isn't," Robbie said, turning to Hope. "Let's get Dandy settled and I'll drive you home, unless you want to come to dinner at the big house? I can guarantee there'll be enough to feed an army."

"Thanks, but I'll hang out at Beth and Lang's, take a long, hot shower, and go to bed early," she said as they walked back outside, leaving Kyle to chat with Ben.

"Love to join you, but duty calls."

"And Janie, too," she whispered as they spied the redhead, untying the last of the horses.

"Don't you start! Give me a few minutes and I'll drive you back."

*****

When the truck pulled up, he cut the engine and turned to her. "Thanks for today. Are you sure you'll be up to riding again tomorrow? I'm not sure I am."

"Panty hose," she said. "I'm a bit tired and sore, but they help a lot."

"I think it's too late for panty hose. The damage is done," he said, giving her a weary grin as he reached over to stroke her chin. "How can you look so beautiful after a day like today? I think I have just enough energy to kiss you, if you'll let me?"

In answer, she leaned over, arms circling his neck, drawing him close. The kiss, sweet and deep, was enough to arouse them both, and as she stroked his thigh, Hope felt the bulge of his penis and sighed. "Oh, my, someone's not as tired as he thought, but I'm not about to give your sister and Lang a show." She stroked him gently at first, then with more insistence.

"Oh, God, Hope, you're trying to kill me, aren't you?" His hands cupped her breasts and he felt ready to explode.

Beth appeared on the porch holding the baby. "Hey, guys! Are you coming in, Robbie? We've got plenty of leftovers if you want supper."

Breaking apart, they laughed as they pulled themselves together. "Thanks, sis," he called, "but I've gotta get back. Give Lily a kiss for me."

Hope hopped out, then poked her head in the window. "Thanks, and I'll let you know about me and tomorrow. If these guys need me, I'll stay behind."

"Night," he said, returning her smile. *I think I'm in love with you.*

CHAPTER 32

"I don't know what to do," Leonora said, head in hands, elbows uncharacteristically slumped on the breakfast table, Ben Senior beside her. "Ruthie loves Christmas! Should we even have the dinner? Oh, my poor, poor baby out in this cold. Where could she be? Where could she be? And now that pushy Jane is in her room. What if they find her today? Where will we put everyone?" She raised her head and gazed over at her husband with her red, puffy eyes.

Ben Senior placed his hand over hers. "Hey, sweetie, it's gonna be okay."

"How do you know that?"

"They'll find her, and Robbie's already blocked rooms at the Lodge if they stay on."

"When?"

"When what?"

"When will they find her? I'll have Carmela make up her room. When will we see our sweet Ruthie?"

"Hopefully today," Robbie said, stepping into the room.

"You off, son?" his father asked.

"Soon as I get the saddle bags from Carmela."

"What about breakfast?" Leonora asked, sitting straighter, pushing wisps of hair from her brow.

"Ate with Kyle an hour ago, Mom." He stooped to kiss her cheek.

"Where is he, anyway?"

"At the stables, helping with the horses."

"And the others?"

"They ate with us, then went into town for supplies. They'll join us at the barn."

Leonora grabbed his arm. "Bring my baby back to me."

"We'll find her, promise." He hugged her, then glanced at his father, whose eyes had filled. While they were all close, Ben Senior had a special bond with Ruthie and they all knew it. She was his buddy and confidante, a relationship forged when she was a toddler.

"Hey, Dad, if we get reception, I'll try to get out a call. Ty's men have walkie-talkies, too. Somehow we'll get word."

"Thanks, son. You take care and tell Ty thanks for joining the search."

"It's his job, for pity's sake," Leonora said, wringing her napkin. County Sheriff Ty Boone had sent two of his men and also put out a call to the horsemen in a local volunteer hiking and riding group. At least three had joined the sheriff's men and were headed for the western foothills and mountains beyond. "When will the helicopter get here?"

"About one thirty or two. They're comin' from Sedona."

"You goin' up with them?" Robbie asked.

His father nodded. "If they'll have me."

"You're paying for them. Of course they'll have you!" his mother said, hugging her son.

Robbie pulled back, giving her a peck on the cheek. "Hey, Mom, we'll find 'em. And you gotta promise that if we don't get home tonight, you'll do Christmas Eve anyway."

"We'll have dinner, but no secret Santa without your sister," his mother said. "Your dad and I already decided that. We'll do something for the little ones, though."

One of their favorite times of the year, Christmas Eve was a big night at the ranch. First they celebrated with the entire staff at a late afternoon party at the

Lodge, the tables groaning with food, drinks flowing. Then the family said their good nights and came home to the big house for soup and sandwiches and a raucous secret Santa gift exchange to end the evening. After a lavish Christmas Day breakfast and gift opening, everyone usually took a ride or walk, then had a sumptuous dinner that evening. This year, along with their immediate family, they had invited Spark Foster, Amy, Jeb, Toby, and the Dillons to join them.

"Okay, well, I'm off," he said and swung open the kitchen door.

"Careful, son!" his father called as Spark Foster stepped in from the front hall. "Mornin', buddy. What brings you out this early?"

"Carmela's breakfast, of course," he said, smiling as he bent to kiss Leonora.

"Of course, join us," she said. "There's plenty. Coffee's hot, too."

"Thanks, Nora, but I'm just kidding. I ate earlier, but I won't say no to coffee." He grabbed one of her brightly colored mugs and poured himself a cup. "Wanted to stop by to discuss something. Any sign of Ruthie?"

Ben shook his head. "What's up?"

"Tonight's shindig at the Lodge still on?"

"Yes, we think it's important for the staff," she said. "Though goodness knows how we're going to hold our heads up and get through it."

"Yer friends'll be there so you can lean on us. You don't have to feed us after, either."

"Nonsense. Carmela's already prepared most of it," she said. "And we hope they'll have found them by then."

"And if they haven't," Ben said, "We'll want you here anyway."

"We'll be there. Toby's about to jump out of his skin with excitement."

"Oh, dear," Leonora said. "That's true. The kids will be so disappointed about the secret Santa." She turned to Spark. "Ben and I decided to postpone until Ruthie's back."

"No worries. I have a bunch of stuff over at my place. I'll bring a few things for Toby and Ben and Maggie's two to open. I don't 'spose little Lily will care about presents yet."

"Oh, Spark," she said, patting his hand. "You are such a dear friend. What did we ever do before you moved to the Valley?"

Spark gazed at his friend's beautiful wife, whom he'd known for over forty years, ever since his college roommate had introduced them. He'd never seen Ben Morgan so crazy about a woman. When they were in the same room, his eyes seldom left her then or now. Ben and Leonora Morgan were the most loving couple he knew, just like him and his Patsy.

Spark cleared his throat, "Nora, Ben, it would be my honor and pleasure to take over tomorrow's dinner. I know what yer gonna say, that Carmela's got that under control, too, but I spoke to her yesterday and she told me where she is. I asked her to stop, freeze things, and bring what she can't freeze. Let me do this for you all. I'm not tryin' to push in or take that tradition away from you. You can have it right back next year, but this year, you've got a lot on your minds."

"And so do you," Leonora said, gazing over at him. "What about the wedding and all the arrangements for next week? Why, you have—"

"Thanks, buddy," her husband interrupted. "We accept."

Leonora opened her mouth to protest, then closed it, smiling through tears at their dear friend. "Guess it's settled. Thank you, dear Spark. I will coordinate everything with Carmela."

"All set. Aria will be over this morning," Spark said, a grin on his face. "Let's let the experts handle the catering and we three can go into town and have lunch at Gracie's."

"Spark, I have a million other things to do…wrapping, decorating. And I may have to pick up Sam and Rose."

"We accept," Ben said. "We'll pick you up around eleven fifteen. I have to be back by one to meet the helicopter. Nora, Lang's picking up the kids, as you well know."

"Gracie's it is," she said, throwing up her hands and smiling for the first time that morning.

Ben watched her, knowing she'd be in tears as soon as Spark departed, but full of gratitude for this brief happy moment when the whereabouts of their precious baby was still unknown.

CHAPTER 33

As Lang and Hope pulled up the stables at sunrise, she turned to him. "Are you sure about this?"

"Absolutely," he said, smiling at her. "My mom'll be here in an hour and I'll be back by ten with Rose and Sam. You know she'll be dying to grab Lily and take over."

"Yeah, right, after taking the red-eye."

"You don't know my sister. She's the only person I know who can sleep like the dead on an airplane."

"Are pharmaceuticals involved?"

He laughed. "Nope, she's been like that since we were kids. Now, get—the gang'll be here soon."

She grabbed a small pack from the back seat and her water bottles. "Thanks, Lang. See you tonight, I hope."

"Good luck."

"We'll need it," she said, turning to spy Kyle Morgan parking one of the ranch trucks.

The thin, dark-haired veterinarian hopped out and tipped his hat. "Mornin', Hope. You're here early."

"Wasn't sure what time you were leaving and I thought I could help with the horses."

"Likewise." He grinned, flashing the Morgan smile, the undoing of many an unsuspecting woman.

"You made a smooth transition from vet to cowboy."

He laughed, grabbing a small pack from the truck. "Almost vet, always a cowboy. Looks like Nick's here. Shall we?"

They strolled through the dark barn, finding Nick Parker in the back, all six horses in the corral behind him, saddled and nickering in the growing light. "Hey," he said, waving. After a quick nod at Kyle, his eyes lingered on Hope.

"We came down to help, brother, but it looks like you're all set."

"Just about. If you're bored there are always the stalls to muck out."

Kyle looked at Hope and she shrugged. "Why not? We're here and it's cold. At least we'll warm up."

Both stripped to tee shirts, grabbed pitchforks and rakes, and headed inside.

CHAPTER 34

By the time Ben, Harley, and Robbie's crew arrived, Hope and Kyle were drenched in sweat, faces smudged with dirt, bits of straw covering them from head to toe. When Robbie spied her, he thought she had never looked lovelier.

Ben grinned. "Never know we're looking at a well-known artist and a doc."

"Where's Janie?" Robbie asked, noticing the redhead was nowhere in sight.

"She went back to the house to make a call," Dave said. "She's thinking about heading back home since you guys are out for two nights and we don't need the ATVs."

Robbie shook his head. Secretly he was relieved to see the back of Jane, whose flirting had been getting old the last few months. Her behavior was one of the reasons he was glad to get out of Sedona and, truth be told, he wasn't eager to return. *What is wrong with the woman? No is no. I've made that quite clear.*

Startled by his gesture, Hope stared at him.

Harley surveyed the group, eyes grave. "Hey, guys, we've gotta roll. You two okay? You better go throw those shirts in the office and grab new ones. There's a whole pile in there. Parker, show 'em, will you?"

They rode out together and split up a mile from the ranch, Kyle, Dave, and Ben headed south, the others east. Midday, Hal and Harley veered off on a southeast trail, leaving Robbie and Hope to take a trail that ran east to the riverbed. It was

Harley's idea. "Won't get lost that way. Stay on it and follow the river. That way, we'll meet up in a couple of hours when the trail loops back."

"But?" Robbie said, eying the wrangler, who had spoken barely a syllable all morning.

"It's one of your sister's favorites. This other is, too."

They rode mostly in silence, their eyes scanning the brown, parched landscape broken only by cactus and tumbleweeds, with a few dead trees and piles of boulders. Occasionally they caught the distant sound of a hawk's cry. The path was wide enough for both horses so they rode side by side, their legs occasionally brushing against each other's. Fortunately, Dandy and Royal got along and the horses often nuzzled noses, nickering softly as they made their way.

Aside from the worry about his lost sister, Robbie realized he had never felt so at peace. Hope's grounded presence made him feel more at home than he'd felt since he left for college. *Not sure where this is going, buddy, but it's sure worth the ride.*

"You okay?" she asked, turning to glimpse a strange expression on his face.

"Yeah, sure, why?"

"You just looked funny, almost like you were sick."

Love-sick, he thought. *How can I even be thinking about myself when Ruthie's out there somewhere?* "No, just worried, that's all. Ruthie's a pain in the neck, but she's never pulled anything like this."

"We'll find her," she said, reaching over to take his hand.

"Thanks, Hope, for being here, for everything," he said, turning away so she wouldn't see the tears in his eyes. *Where the hell are they coming from?*

But she had seen them, and if Hope had had any doubt before, she knew with certainty that she was hopelessly head over heels in love with Robbie Morgan. "Wanta stop? Take a break, give the horses water and rest?"

He turned back to give her a warm smile, dry-eyed now. "No, we better keep moving. We'll be at the foothills soon. There'll be some shade."

*****

They reached the trailhead before the others and slid off the horses, bone-tired and discouraged. "Jesus Christ," he said, groaning, one leg half asleep, needles of pain coursing through it. "Not sure I'll be able to get back up."

"Walk around a bit. Shake your legs. It'll work itself out."

He groaned again. "Not what I've got, babe. I feel about a hundred."

"Me, too."

"Liar."

"Come over here and sit on this rock."

He sat, gazing up quizzically. "We've got to water the horses, you know."

Eyes twinkling with mischief, she smiled down at him. "They're fine. This'll only take a few minutes." She stooped and began massaging his calves, her strong hands kneading the knotted muscles, loosening them. She then moved to his knees and thighs, her magic fingers bringing relief and comfort. Robbie sighed, leaning back, marveling at the amazing woman in front of him.

"Oh, my God, Hope, that feels great," he said as her hands moved toward his groin. Before he knew it, he felt himself grow hard. She noticed but kept stroking, fingers swirling around the tops of his legs, caressing his hips.

He grinned sheepishly. "Didn't think I had it in me."

"What? An adventurer like you?"

Hope smiled as he stroked her chin, then cupped it, intending to lean closer to kiss her when he heard voices as Harley and Hal came into view.

"Hey, buddy," Hal called. "We aren't interrupting anything, are we?"

Hope jumped up, face beet red.

Robbie grabbed his hat to cover his lap. "This woman has magic fingers. She was attempting to ease my screaming muscles."

One eyebrow raised, Harley eyed the hat. "We've all been there, Morgan. Think you can ride?"

"Sure, not a problem, but we should give the horses water."

"Glad to see you have your priorities straight," Harley said. "These horses need to get us home, you know."

Robbie turned his back on the wrangler, grabbing one of the water bags. *After this is all over, I'm gonna get no end of shit for this. Wait'll my brothers hear about it.*

CHAPTER 35

As the sun sank lower in the sky, the four pressed onward, climbing a twisting trail that led through the mountains. Midway up, they reached a clearing about thirty feet square with scraggly moss-covered rocks and patches of scrub grass. "This is far enough," Harley said, dismounting and letting Pepper free. Always watchful and wary, the horse rarely took her eyes off her owner and was never more than ten feet from Harley.

As the others dismounted and tethered their horses near the patches of grass, Harley gazed at a narrow path to the east of them. "You all settle in. I'm gonna walk up and see if I can spot 'em from the ridge."

"You're pretty sure they came this way, then?" Robbie asked, taking tentative steps on wobbly legs.

The wrangler nodded, grabbing a water bottle and binoculars from his pack.

"I'll come with you," Hal said. "Be good to stretch my legs."

"I'm happy to go," Robbie said.

"No, you stay here with Hope and the horses," Harley said. "There're mountain lions and coyote up here. Don't want to spook 'em. 'Sides, it'll give you two time for another lap dance." He grinned as he patted Pepper. "You stay here, Pepp. Watch out for the others."

Robbie shook his head, looking over at Hope. "Don't you start!"

She smiled, patting his shoulder. "Come on, cowboy. Let's get this campsite together. Can we make a fire?"

"Small one. There's lots of tinder around here, but wood? Not so much."

"We passed some debris back a ways. I'll go grab it."

"Be careful. No, on second thought, don't go. There's enough around here and mountain lions prefer lone targets."

They worked quietly until they gathered a pile of wood, sticks, and brush. After lighting the fire, they pulled out food and laid camp, their bedrolls as close to the fire as possible. As they stood back to survey their work, Hope shivered.

"You cold?" he asked.

"A little. I'm looking at those thin bedrolls and wondering if I'll survive. I forgot how cold it can get in the mountains."

"No worries. We'll share body heat."

Hope raised an eyebrow.

"No funny business, promise. Don't want to give Harley anything else to blab to my brothers."

She laughed. "Now who's talking about funny business?"

As darkness descended, Robbie lit the fire and they prepared a simple dinner of the chili and bread that Carmela had packed. Hope was stirring the pot when Harley and Hal returned, covered with dust and looking bone-tired, their expressions grave.

Robbie asked, "Anything?"

Harley shook his head. "Nothing."

Hope watched the tall, handsome wrangler, and for a second she thought she spied tears in his eyes. Hal joined them around the fire, and she handed him a bowl of chili topped with a thick slab of cornbread. Harley checked the horses, spent a few minutes talking softly to Pepper, then joined them, nodding as she handed him a steaming bowl.

Shortly after dinner, they retired, Hal and Harley to one side of the fire, Robbie and Hope on the other. By then the night air had dropped to what felt like freezing. Deciding she didn't care what the others thought, Hope slipped into her bedroll, then scooted up against Robbie. He circled his arms round her, his warmth seeping into her. "Is this okay?" she whispered.

In answer, he kissed the top of her head. "More than okay, even without the funny business."

Hope smiled, burrowing into his strong shoulder, pressing her body against him, his erection tickling her tummy. "Hmm…" she murmured, "Too bad we're not alone."

"Sleep, sweetheart," he whispered. "Probably couldn't act on it, anyway."

Her eyelids heavy, she gazed across the fire, spying Harley, wide awake, back against a rock. He looked as if he hadn't slept in two days, which was probably true, and she doubted he would sleep tonight.

CHAPTER 36

After services in the village chapel, a solemn group gathered at the big house. Spark, Amy, Jeb, and Toby arrived first, soon followed by Ben, the kids, Maggie, and her dad.

Spark hugged Leonora, then turned to his friend. "Hey, buddy. How long were you up?"

"Chopper got here at two and we were out most of the afternoon."

"No sign?"

"No, and we covered a lot of ground."

"They may have taken shelter."

"That's what we're hoping. The pilot's staying at the Lodge. We'll go back up first thing."

"Need another pair of eyes?"

"Thanks, but they can only take one more and Sam's going with me."

"Good." Spark hugged his dear friend, who looked frail and shaky.

After showering and unpacking, Sam and Rose drove up with her parents. Beth, Lang, and Lily came last, the baby in a fuzzy sling on her father's chest.

"No word?" Lang asked as they hugged Leonora and Ben in the front hall.

"Ben called an hour ago, but no sign of 'em. They're about to hunker down for the night."

"Oh, my poor baby," Leonora said. "It's so cold tonight."

"Ruthie knows what she's doing, Mama," Beth said, hugging her mother. "She's a survivor."

"But what about him? What do we really know about Kevin? Nothing, that's what!"

As they made their way in to join the others, Ben Senior circled his arm round his daughter's shoulders. "We spoke to his folks today. They're in Denver, waiting to hear news. They're planning to wait another day, then head this way. His dad says Kevin's an experienced hiker. He knows the mountains."

"But not these mountains," Leonora said, putting on a smile as they faced the children. "Now, babies, what kind of mischief are you getting into? Anyone want a present?"

"We do, we do!" Emma and Toby shouted.

"Me do, me do," Ben the third chimed in.

"Well, then, you shall have one, precious things!"

The adults watched as Emma, Toby, and Ben unwrapped a few gifts and began playing with robots, dolls, a jack-in-the-box and several soft balls. Emma opened a game called "Spot It," which she and Toby went off to play with Ned in the adjoining study while Ben rolled balls around the living room.

"We're lucky, aren't we?" Spark said. "These are some cute kids."

Ben Senior nodded at his dear friend, then gazed at his wife, tears streaking her beautiful cheeks. "And our sons are gonna bring our cute kid home, darlin'." In his heart, he knew their baby was okay and that Ben, Kyle, Robbie, and the others would find her.

For the children's sake, they all made an attempt at cheerfulness, even the usually taciturn Jaybo Dillon. His less than affable moods were due to poor health and too much alcohol, but tonight he seemed to perk up, joining in the merriment for the sake of the children and their dear friends and neighbors. Martha held Lily most of the evening, and the smile on Jaybo's face when he gazed over at grandmother and child was heartwarming.

Carmela served individual ice cream treats in the shape of Christmas trees, wreaths, candy canes, Santa Claus, and brightly lit candles. Made in antique molds that had been passed down through the Morgan family, they were a Christmas tradition. *No one loves them more than Ruthie,* Sam thought, watching his parents' efforts to be merry.

"Hey, you," Rose said, slipping her arm round his waist. "Don't know about you, but the red-eye has caught up to me. Dad's starting to fade, too."

"I think everyone needs to turn in," he said, kissing the top of her head. "I'll start the ball rolling."

Ned helped Maggie get Emma and Ben packed up as Lang and Beth said their good nights. Sam and Rose helped Jaybo to the car, then he came back in to say good night. "Mom, Dad, you gonna be okay? This was poor planning on our part. We should have stayed with you guys first."

"We're fine, son," his father said, hugging him. "Give us somethin' to look forward to next week."

"Night, honey," Leonora said, kissing him. "It's so good to have you home."

Ben and Leonora stepped onto the porch, waving as the others drove away. A clear, starry sky stretched in front of them. She shivered and he drew her close. "My poor, poor baby out on this cold night."

"Remember, darlin' that Ruthie is almost impervious to cold. She's always been the one in a bathing suit in January."

Leonora blew several kisses into the darkness. "Sleep tight, sweetheart, wherever you are. Your brothers are coming."

CHAPTER 37

"Merry Christmas, campers!" Harley called in the semidarkness. "Time to get cracking." He had the fire going and was toasting slabs of bread, with pouches of peanut butter and honey nearby.

Robbie sat up and squinted. Every fiber of his body ached. "Hey, Harl."

"Not the usual Morgan Christmas breakfast, but it'll have to do. I want to get going soon."

"Which way?"

"I have an idea, which means backtracking. We forgot Lobo Canyon. It's another one of your sister's favorites, just south of here. If they're there, we wouldn't see any trace of 'em until we enter the canyon."

"Wasn't Ben headed that way?"

"Maybe. You wake Sleeping Beauty and I'll rouse Hal."

The group made their way slowly downward, the terrain rocky and dangerous with hairpin turns and narrow paths along the ridge. Robbie followed Hope, the last of the riders, watching the gentle way she guided her horse, always keeping Dandy calm and steady. If he had to guess, Jaybo Dillon's horse had not seen terrain like this in many years—Royal, either. The older generation rarely rode and when they did, it was not in the mountains.

As they descended, the temperature warmed and Hope wished she dared loosen the reins long enough to remove her jacket. *Better to sweat and live than to plunge off this cliff,* she decided. Harley letting go to fling off his coat was one thing as he and Pepper rode as one, but she didn't know Dandy well enough to chance it.

After several hours, Harley called, "Almost down, folks. Be easier from here."

Hal reined in his horse and fumbled in his pocket. "I've got a ping!" he called, extracting the walkie-talkie. The group paused, waiting. "It's Dave," he called. "They're about six miles from here. The chopper's spotted something near Lobo."

"I knew it! Tell 'em we're headed their way. Probably be there in an hour or so," Harley said.

"And, call the ranch, will you?" Robbie said. "Let the family know we're okay."

"Your dad and brother are in the chopper so they've probably already let 'em know."

As they rode into the open desert, Harley lifted binoculars.

"Can you see 'em?" Robbie asked, coming up beside him. "Looks like dust?"

Harley continued to stare for several minutes, then dropped the binoculars into his saddle bag. "It's not dust. It's smoke. Someone's out there just east of Lobo. The chopper's already there. Let's go."

With that, he nudged Pepper and the powerful horse took off at a gallop, Hal and the others behind him. Hope turned to Robbie, eyes full of concern. "Is that wise? I mean, look where we are. At this point, isn't caution safer with snakes and all?"

"It's Ruthie," he said, shaking his head. "Always been crazy in love with her, the foolish bastard. Come on. We don't have to ride like that."

"Oh, yes we do, cowboy. Safest place now is in Langdon's wake. Come on!" Hope nudged Dandy and off she flew.

"Jesus Christ," Robbie said, urging Royal onward. His father's horse hesitated for a moment, then took off. *If the rattlers don't kill me, this ride and that woman will!*

They reached Harley and Hal just as Ben, Kyle, and Dave rode up. It took a moment to adjust to what they were seeing. Kevin Statler sat glassy-eyed, huddled near a small fire, no sign of Ruthie. The pilot, Ben Senior, and Sam Morgan stood over him. Kevin wore only a tee shirt, with no jacket. As they approached, he did not appear to notice them, but stared at the fire, eyes vacant. Their horses were also missing.

"What's going on?" Harley called.

"Damndest thing," Ben Senior said. "No one can get a word outta the kid. She can't be too far, but where are the horses?"

Harley leaped from Pepper. "Hey, Statler!" The other man did not look up or respond, so Harley grabbed hold of him, dragging him to his feet and shaking him. "Statler, look at me!"

No response.

The wrangler slapped him hard across the face, then went back to shaking him. Ben and Robbie came to their side, Ben grabbed Harley and Robbie caught Statler as he fell.

"Hey, buddy," Ben said. "Leave him alone."

Harley eyes blazed. "Not till he tells me where she is!"

Hal placed a hand on his shoulder. "He's in shock, man."

Harley shrugged from his grasp. "Like I give a shit."

Ben Senior stepped forward. "Son, he's not gonna tell us a goddamn thing if you knock him out. Now, step back."

Hope wet her bandana and knelt, placing it on Kevin's dry, dusty lips. "Hey, Kevin, you're safe now."

Statler threw himself at her, sobbing uncontrollably. "I'm sorry, I'm sorry. I tried to help her…I tried. Couldn't reach her."

"You're okay," she said, softly, patting his back. "We need to find Ruthie. Do you know where she is?"

"She can't be far," Kyle said, exchanging looks with the others. It was clear from all their expressions that they feared the worst.

Harley took a step forward.

"Back up, buddy," Ben said. "Let him settle down."

Robbie squatted in front of him. "Hey, Kev, 'member me?"

Statler nodded.

"Well, I've been riding for two days to find you and my sister. We've got the helicopter here to bring you home, but we can't go anywhere without Ruthie. Comprende?"

Kevin nodded blankly.

"This isn't getting us anywhere," Harley said, pacing a short distance away. "I'm gonna ride into Lobo." He leaped onto Pepper and turned southeast.

"No," Kevin said.

"Hold on, buddy," Ben called as he knelt beside Robbie. "You know somethin' Kev? Where we can find her?"

Kevin raised an arm and pointed east to a mountainous area less than a mile away.

"Jesus Christ, Devil's Dome," Harley said. "That's why the choppers didn't spot her. Why the hell is this bastard out here?"

"Maybe he came out to build the fire to attract attention," Robbie said.

"Yeah, right. He looks like a resourceful kind of guy."

"Harley, wait," Ben called as the others headed for the horses.

"You okay?" Robbie asked, gazing at Hope.

"Go," she said, giving him a wan smile.

"I'd like to come," Sam said. "You guys mind?" He gazed over at Hal and Dave.

"No problem, man. Dave and I'll stay back." Hal said. "Take my horse. We've got medical supplies. Hope, you should go with them. Looks like they're gonna need good riders if they're heading up there. No telling what you'll find."

"Here, brother," he said, throwing Robbie a coil of rope, then one of the walkie-talkies. "Good luck."

CHAPTER 38

"What's Devil's Dome?" Hope called as they followed the others across the barren ground, headed for a narrow, cliff-lined trail that led straight up.

"It's a weird outcropping of rock that hangs forty feet over the trail. I always hated it as a kid. Freaked me out. Looked like it was gonna fall on us. Freaked us all out, except Ruthie."

They hadn't climbed far when they spied Ruthie's pinto, Jadie, and a stable horse, Annie, grazing in a small patch of grass at the side of the trail. Twenty feet farther and they rode under an enormous dome of rock. Harley reined Pepper and jumped from the saddle. To his left was a sharp crevice running along the southern edge, a dark, open wound in the rock. As the others reached him, each peered down, spying a clump of bedding and clothing.

"Ruthie!" Harley called, already scanning the cliff to find a way downward, his eyes wild. "Ruthie, we're here! Can you hear me?"

They all began calling her name to no avail. The pile remained still. The sheer cliff face offered no visible means of descent. "Oh, Robbie," Hope said, hand on his arm, watching the still pile of debris below them.

"She's alive. I know it," Harley muttered to himself. "Gotta get down there. Get the ropes."

"I'll go down," Ben said.

"Like hell you will," Harley said, already tying a rope around his waist.

"She's my sister."

"This is my fault, not yours."

"Bullshit. Now take off that damn rope and give it to me!"

"She moved!" Hope cried, peering below. "She's alive! Ruthie!"

Ben looked down. "We're comin', sis! Hang on!" He turned back to Harley, voice softer. "Listen, buddy, you're stronger than me. They'll need you up here."

Harley shook his head. "Pepp'll pull us up. Hurry, now."

Ben exchanged glances with his brothers, then said, "Okay, everyone, let's do this. Be careful, buddy."

As they slowly lowered him down, Harley fought for a purchase on the smooth rock face. Mostly he hung helplessly as he descended into the dark crevasse. She lay on a narrow ledge. Another foot and she would have fallen beyond their reach. Harley bent over her and gently removed the clothes and bedding, checking her for injuries. They could not hear what was said, but finally Ruthie managed to place weak arms around his neck as Harley lifted her into his arms. He held her to him, gently smoothing hair from her brow before gazing upward. "She's okay! Leg's broken! Get us outta here. Very slowly, guys!"

When they reached the top, Harley handed her to Ben.

"Merry Christmas, Shortcake," he said, taking his sister from Harley's arms as Robbie, Kyle, and Sam assisted.

Hope helped Harley remove the harness. He was shaking and when she looked up, she saw tears in his eyes.

Mud-covered and weak, Ruthie gave her oldest brother a wan smile. "Don't call me that, you big jerk. What took you guys so long, anyway?"

"She's okay," Ben said, grinning as the others swooped in to hug her.

As Robbie joined the melee, he gazed over, spying Harley's tear-streaked face. *Kevin Statler better have a good excuse for leaving her here or this cowboy's gonna tar and feather him.*

Hope watched the brothers embrace their baby sister and marveled again at the loving bond between them. Robbie caught her eye and she smiled. *What a lucky man you are, Robbie Morgan.*

CHAPTER 39

They unloaded gear and supplies to lighten the helicopter's load so that Ben Senior could accompany Ruthie and Kevin to Valley Hospital. The others headed home, arriving in the early evening. Spark had asked Aria to wrap Christmas dinner, and she and Carmela had worked together to set out a huge feast at the big house. Dehydrated and ill, Kevin Statler elected to stay overnight at the hospital. His parents were on their way from Colorado to join him there.

After her leg was set and they pumped fluids into her, Ruthie insisted on coming home. She and her parents arrived just as the weary riders reached the ranch. Lang, Jeb, Nick, and Jane waited to tend to the horses. As Robbie and Hope rode into the yard, Jane waved. "Surprise—I'm still here! Couldn't leave till I knew my main man was safe."

Hope slipped from the saddle, smiling as Lang caught her. She held onto his shoulders for a minute to get her bearings. "Thanks. I wasn't sure I'd be able to stand."

"You okay now? I can carry you to the Rover?"

She laughed. "Absolutely not! Your brother-in-law may need help, though."

"Not from what I'm looking at," he whispered, gazing over her shoulder.

Hope turned to find Jane Mackenzie, arm round Robbie's waist, half carrying him toward the barn, cooing in his ear. Too tired to care, Hope patted Lang's arm. "I'll wait in the Rover. You help the others." Without a backward glance, she headed through the barn to the jeep. Once inside the Rover, she closed her eyes. *This is the price for falling in love with a guy like Robbie Morgan. There's always going to be a Jane Mackenzie hanging around.*

"Hey," he said softly, his voice startling her.

Hope realized she had fallen asleep and gave him a startled look. "Oh!" She noticed that Jane was still glued to his side.

"You want to ride with us?" he asked, prompting a scowl from his companion.

"No thanks. Here comes Lang. I'm good."

He placed a hand over hers. "See you at the house, then?"

"Of course," she said. "After a long, hot shower."

Pulling away from Jane, he leaned in and kissed her cheek. "Thanks, Hope. You promise you're coming?"

She reached up and ran her fingers along his strong jaw. "Go. I'll see you soon."

CHAPTER 40

Carmela and Aria outdid themselves with the food and everyone had pitched in with the decorations. Leonora had the men bring tables from the barns and cellar and place them everywhere to accommodate the large crowd. There were tables set up in the study and library. The dining room table was decked out with the family's traditional Christmas regalia—plates, linens, and lovely floral arrangements—while the extra tables were a riot of color with brightly patterned linens and Leonora's beautiful collection of pottery.

"Can't believe you pulled this off, Nora," Spark said, giving her a hug as he and his family arrived.

"*We* pulled it off, dear Spark," she said, returning his embrace. "Hey, Amy, Jeb, and there's my sweetheart, Toby!" She scooped the redhead from his wheelchair and swung him around. Still tiny for his age, Toby was light as a feather but healthy, his cheeks rosy, eyes shining with happiness at the love of his new parents and proud grandfather.

"Oh, and look who's right behind you!" their hostess said. "It's your cousin, Lily. Come in, come in, you four," she said as Lang, Beth, and Hope came in. Lang held the car seat where Lily slept, bundled up like a sausage.

"Mom, shh!" Beth said, fingers to her lips. "She just went to sleep and she's been kind of fussy today."

"Okay, Toby, you go to Grandpa," Leonora said, handing the child to Spark. "Lang, put her in your dad's study. It'll be relatively quiet until we all sit down to eat. We can find another spot then if needed."

Ben, Maggie, and the kids were in the huge living room festooned with laurels, an enormous tree and all manner of Christmas decorations. Kyle was pretending to be a tiger, chasing after little Ben, and Robbie was chatting with Emma. Pillows propping her up, Ruthie looked like a queen in her father's huge leather recliner. As Spark and Toby stepped into the room and Emma jumped up, hugging him. "Come on, Tobe. Uncle Robbie's gonna play a game with us, aren't you?" She gave her uncle a beautiful smile.

"Course I am! Any more takers?" He gazed around the room and spotted his sister and Hope waving. "Hey, ladies, wanta play?"

"Not now, sweeties. Maybe in a few minutes," Beth said, guiding Hope toward the library. "Let's at least get a drink before we step into that chaos. The doctor said I can have one glass of wine or a beer. What about you?"

"I'd kill for a nice red wine."

"Come on then!" Beth said, leading her across the hall to the library with its dark paneling and book-lined walls.

"Wow!"

Beth smiled. "My favorite room in the house. It's always been my sanctuary. I'd come here to escape from my brothers and the melee."

"It's beautiful. The door has always been closed when I've visited. I never knew what was in here." She gazed around at the leather sofas and chairs, thick Persian rug, and soft lighting. Tonight the furniture was pushed against the far wall to accommodate a round table set for eight. The bar was just inside the door on a sideboard.

"Yes, it's nice. When they built the house, Mom insisted on this room to remind her of home. Apparently her parents' house had one just like it, although it's always looked more like it belongs in an English country house than an Art Deco Hollywood mansion."

"Your mom lived in LA?"

"Santa Barbara. Her dad was a very successful agent. Represented some big stahhs. We never knew him. My grandparents both died in a plane crash right after Mom and Dad were married."

"Hey, ladies," Sam Morgan said, stepping into the room. "What're you doin' hiding out in here?"

"We're not hiding out," Beth said, hugging and kissing her brother. "Where's Rose?"

"With Mom and Martha. Jaybo didn't feel like coming. Just as well. Now Martha can relax and enjoy herself. No Raoul behind the bar tonight?"

"He's a bit busy at the moment," Beth said.

"What can I get you two?" he asked, flashing the gorgeous Morgan smile.

When they returned to the living room, Beth and Sam were swallowed up in the raucous group. The Sedona crew had arrived, as had Nick Parker and Harley. The four men stood, beers in hand, watching the craziness, but Jane was nowhere in sight. Robbie, Emma, and Toby were playing a board game that seemed to involve a great deal of shouting and jumping up and down. Hope knew that Robbie and Emma had a special bond, but she could see how much Toby adored him, as well.

"Hey, Hope. How're your saddle sores?" She turned to find Jane Mackenzie behind her, dressed in black leggings, five-inch heels, and a blue velvet tunic with a plunging neckline. Sexy, perhaps, but somehow the outfit was not flattering. Her red hair was loose, falling around her shoulders, and she wore glittery eye shadow and bright red lipstick.

"Sore," she said, smiling at the other woman.

The heels meant that they now stood eye to eye since Hope wore flats with her gray slacks. She had borrowed one of Beth's sweaters, a soft gray-green cashmere, and accented it with a simple silver necklace and matching earrings.

"You decided to stay on, then?" she asked.

"Snowing hard in Sedona. I didn't want to slog through it. Yikes, this eggnog is strong. Have you tried it?"

Beth laughed. "I had a very unfortunate incident with eggnog in high school and have abstained ever since."

"Smart," Jane said. "Anyway, I'm glad I stayed. Wouldn't have missed this for the world. What a family. What a place."

"Yes."

"This is the largest gathering of drop-dead handsome cowboys I've ever seen in my life."

Hope smiled. "Yes, there is that, too."

"Take your pick, ladies," Aria said as she offered them a tray of appetizers. "And I'm not talking about the food. By my count, at least four or five of them are single, hot, and available."

"No one touches, Robbie," Jane said, taking a gulp of her drink.

"No worries," Aria said, winking at Hope. "I'm kind of partial to the tall, dark ones. And Harley Langdon is to die for."

Jane frowned. "Isn't he like caught up in some lifelong love affair with Ruthie? Hope?"

"Don't ask me. I just got here a few days ago."

"Too bad for you guys that several of the hunks will be leaving soon," Jane said. "Right after the wedding, Robbie's gotta hot foot it back to Sedona. Look at that—isn't he great with kids?"

Aria followed her gaze. "I'd have a kid with him any day and twice on Sunday. Think of how adorable they'd be."

Jane drained her eggnog cup and plunked it on the hall table. "Back off, lady. As I told you, he's spoken for,"

"Well, pardon me. I'll have to settle for Parker. He's pretty cute, too." With that, the chef sashayed off, wending her way across the living room to where Nick and the others stood.

Jane disappeared to find another drink, and Hope watched as Robbie grabbed Emma. It appeared that she had just won the game and he was tickling her in mock dismay. Delighted shrieks and giggles drowned out adult conversation as

Toby joined the melee and the three of them began rolling around the floor. This attracted the attention of baby Ben, who toddled over and sat on Robbie's head. Hope gazed at them sadly, realizing that her companions were right. He was great with kids and would make beautiful ones with someone. *Not me, though. I can't give him that.*

"Hey, darlin', you look like you just lost your best friend," Ben Senior said, arm circling her shoulders. "Can I get you anything?"

"No, thanks, Mr. Morgan. Just tired, I guess."

"Missing home, are you?"

"No, I'm honored to be celebrating with your wonderful family."

"Quite a bunch, aren't they?" he said, gazing across the room, a huge grin on his handsome face. "Gets a bit noisy, but we love it. Nothin' better than havin' the whole brood together, and to have our Ruthie home. Thanks for all your help with that. Your horsemanship came in mighty handy."

"Don't know about that. I have to admit, this rider's having a little trouble sitting tonight."

"Want me to have Carmela put a special cushion on your chair? We have some of those donut things around somewhere."

"Don't you dare! That would be so embarrassing!"

"Well, it's good to have you here. Means the world to Beth and to all of us."

"It's my pleasure. It's given me a nice break from Tucson."

"Had any time for your painting?"

"Not yet, but once things settle down, I should have some time. Truth be told, much as I love it, it's nice to take a break from that, too."

"You do beautiful work, young lady. Sometime after things quiet down, I want to talk to you about a commission. I'd like to give my bride a painting for our fortieth next year."

"I'd be happy to talk about it. Do you have an idea of what you'd like?"

"Still thinkin'," he whispered. "The walls have ears, so I don't want to discuss it tonight. Never know when my Nora'll sneak up on me."

"Like now?" the hostess said, coming from behind to slip her arms around his waist. As she did so, she winked over at Hope.

"See?" he said, turning to embrace her. "What's up, sweetheart?"

"Dinner. We need to eat now before that dreadful Mackenzie woman passes out. She's had too much eggnog and is already slurring. So rude! And the way she throws herself at Robbie! It's disgusting. Honestly, your son is a wimp. Why doesn't he put her in her place?"

"Maybe he has. Some women just don't listen," her husband said, winking at Hope.

"Ha, ha. Hope, you'd better stake your territory before that hussy moves in."

"Excuse me?"

"Our son's crazy about you. Isn't he, Ben? You're all he ever talks about, for goodness' sake. Come on, sweetheart, let's get this dinner started. Spark's hungry and so am I."

With that, Leonora dragged her husband off, leaving Hope slack-jawed. Robbie caught her eye at that moment and gave her what she liked to think was his secret smile, bestowed only on her. She smiled back, heart aching with sadness. *Time to step back. This man deserves so much more. Maybe not Aria Fiorelli or Jane Mackenzie, but a woman who can bear his children—beautiful, perfect Morgan children.*

CHAPTER 41

Carmela and Aria laid out the buffet on the long, narrow farm table in the kitchen. A carved Christmas goose was at one end, slices of beef tenderloin on a huge platter at the other, and in between, pans of roasted vegetables and scalloped potatoes, bowls of green salads, and baskets of freshly baked rolls and breads. Aria had also poached two wild salmon, which she served with baby peas and a light dill sauce.

The elder Morgans, Spark, Martha Dillon, and Ned Williams, sat with the children and Jeb, Amy, Raoul, and Carmela at the dining room table. The others took plates heaped with food to the library or study. Robbie and Hope joined Beth, Lang, Rose, and Sam in the library. After settling the children at the main table, Ben and Maggie stepped in, taking the last two seats.

Ben set down his plate, gazed around, then looked across the hall to the study where Harley was just taking a seat directly across from his baby sister. "Hey, guys, I think I'll switch places with Dave," he said, bending to kiss Maggie's cheek. "Sorry, babe. You okay with this? Don't want to see Christmas turn into a blood bath. "

Maggie smiled up at him. "Go referee! I'll be fine." She turned back to the others. "He's afraid that now Harley knows Ruthie is safe and sound, he might kill her."

"When is he going to give up and tell her how he feels?" Rose asked.

"Worked for me," Sam said, taking Rose's hand.

"Hey, Morgan, when you gonna make my sister an honest woman, anyway?" Lang asked.

"Stop it, Lang!" Rose said, blushing crimson.

"We're thinking next July if we can get the time off. Rose practically lives at the clinic and I've got a monster workload right now, but we're trying to carve out at least four weeks to come home."

Six months earlier, Rose and Sam had moved east, where he joined one of the city's top architectural firms and she took over as director of the Heavers Children's Medical Center where she carried on the work of her gravely ill mentor, Dr. Chris Heavers.

Robbie slipped his hand under the tablecloth, finding Hope's. He felt her stiffen, then relax as he stroked her long, delicate fingers, twining them in his own.

Hope knew she should pull away, but she missed him.

Maggie was staring at her, and Hope blushed, realizing that she had been talking to her. "I'm sorry, daydreaming."

"I know the feeling," Maggie said, soft eyes studying the woman her brother-in-law was obviously crazy about. "I just asked how you were feeling?"

"Better. A little saddle sore, but okay. Just glad everybody's home safe."

"Ben tells me that you're an amazing rider."

"Don't know about amazing, but I enjoy it."

"She's amazing, trust me," Dave said, sitting down in Ben's place. "Left us all in the dust." He took a bite of roast beef and groaned with pleasure. "Do you guys eat like this all the time?"

Maggie laughed. "Only on Christmas. Although Carmela's cooking is pretty incredible, and tonight we've got Spark's Aria, chef extraordinaire, as well. Together, they've really spoiled us."

"And you haven't seen the Yule logs yet," Robbie said, smiling at his colleague.

Dave grinned, blue eyes sparkling. "Bring 'em on!"

"How are they treating you at the Lodge?" Robbie asked.

"Great. Gonna be tough returning to real life tomorrow. Nick was tellin' us that you sometimes get movie stars out here."

Maggie laughed. "Don't mention movie stars to Harley or my husband or you'll get your head bitten off."

Dave gave Robbie a quizzical look.

Robbie grinned at his partner. "Let's just say that some of the stars have been a bit demanding."

Rose gazed over at Hope and smiled. "Beth and Lang are so lucky to have you. How long are you planning to stay?"

"Forever, if we can persuade her," Beth said. "We have our big new house and it's great to have someone *finally* in it!"

"Give it a few years and a bunch of kids'll fill up fast enough," Robbie said.

"Yes, but there will *always* be room for Hope," his sister said, patting her friend's hand.

Hope gulped. *Bunches of kids I'll never have.* "It's been lovely to be here, but I wouldn't want to outstay my welcome. I'll probably head back to Tucson in a month or two, whenever my nannying duties are over."

"Try twelve years," Lang said, winking at her.

"Your parents' day care cottage should be up soon."

"I'd guess summer," Maggie said. "Sam, aren't you doing the plans?"

"Got 'em," her brother said. "They're Mom and Dad's Christmas present. You'll see 'em later."

*****

One of the family's most treasured traditions was the presentation of the Yule logs. A call to the dining room went out and everyone gathered around the sideboard, where Carmela had set three platters of Yule logs, with silver pitchers of chocolate sauce and bowls of whipped cream beside them. Aria had made dozens of Christmas cookies, baskets of which were placed on the tables. Silver pots of coffee and tea were at either end of the buffet.

"Merry Christmas, everyone!" Leonora cried, standing arm in arm with her husband. "We hope you left room for dessert!"

"Oh, my goodness," Hope said.

"Totally over the top," Beth whispered, "but wait till you taste them."

They stood at the edge of the group, watching as the others served themselves and returned to the tables. At one point, Harley stepped forward and asked Ruthie if he could help with her plate, but she gave him a curt no and turned away, chin jutted out, hobbling on one crutch to her seat.

Beth sighed. "Oh, dear, I fear there was trouble at dinner."

"Ya think?" Robbie asked, coming up between them, draping an arm on each of their shoulders.

It felt good to be a part of this loving family, even for a brief time. Hope leaned against him, enjoying the moment, until she looked across the room to find Jane Mackenzie glaring at her.

CHAPTER 42

A raucous secret Santa gift exchange followed dessert. Each person had drawn a name and filled a small stocking with lighthearted gifts. Spark and his crew and Martha Dillon had been included this year, and Harley always took part. With Martha's help, Leonora had made up stockings for all the guests, as well. Everyone contributed to the children's stockings, so they were kept busy opening and playing with a bounty of small gifts.

"When are those two going to grow up?" Robbie whispered as they helped clean up mountains of wrapping paper and ribbons.

"Who?" Hope said, meeting his eyes. There was a softness there now as he looked at her.

"My spoiled sister and Harley. If Dad and Spark hadn't been between them, they'd probably have started a brawl."

"I should think it would be just the opposite. After all, he did save her," she whispered.

"Ruthie's a hothead. What can I say?"

"Hey, stranger." Jane draped her arm around his shoulder. "Have barely seen you all night."

"Hey, Janie," he said as he wiggled out of her embrace, bending to grab a trash bag. "Oh, no you don't, partner. The guys and I are leaving in the morning. Come sit and have a drink with me." She turned to Hope. "You don't mind, do you, hon?"

Hope smiled. "Not at all, but I could do without the 'hon.'"

"Good to know. Come on, you," Jane said, dragging Robbie toward the bar.

Hope waved as he looked back, mouthing "sorry."

"Okay, everyone, come gather round!" Leonora called, clapping her hands. "Sam has something special to show us!"

Hope went to stand next to Beth, who had Lily in a front pack. Lang was beside her, arm round her shoulders. When all had gathered in the living room, Sam held up two large display boards on which he had mounted architectural drawings. "My Christmas gift to Mom and Dad."

One board showed a rendering of the beautiful renovated cottage and surrounding play area. The other was a plan for interior space.

"Oh, Sam, you've outdone yourself," Maggie said. "What a beautiful place. Aren't our children lucky?"

"And there are places for grandparents to come and sit while enjoying our sweethearts." Leonora said. "Ned, come look."

"Mighty nice, Nora," Maggie's dad said.

"What's the timeline for construction?" Ben asked as Emma jumped up and down.

"They'll break ground in March," his father said. "The building will be moved as soon as the foundation's in. With Larrabee's crew, it should be ready by summer."

"Oh, Toby, look," Amy said, pointing to the play yard.

Jeb stooped beside their son. "What'd you think, buddy? Wanta give it a try here on the ranch?"

Toby smiled and nodded. "Can I bring my toys?"

"Darlin', you can bring any darn thing you want," Leonora said, bending to hug him. "Can't he, Granddad?"

"You betcha," Spark said, beaming. "We're gonna make sure there are plenty of toys there, too, aren't we?"

"Absolutely," Leonora said.

Ben Senior draped his arm around her shoulders. "And just so everyone knows, this project is now a joint effort between Ned, Spark, and us. Our fellow grandparents strong-armed their way in, and Nora and I could not be happier."

Everyone crowded round to ooh and aah at the plans. Hope noticed that Jane stayed glued to Robbie, now resting her head on his shoulder as she peeked over to look.

"What's her problem?" Beth whispered. "Is she drunk?"

Hope smiled. "Territorial, I think."

"You okay? You look tired, sweetie," Lang said, arm round his wife.

"I'm fine, but you are right, mother hen. I'm pooped. I think it's safe for us to slip away now. Hope, you can stay if you'd like. Someone'll be happy to drive you home."

"I'd rather go back to the house, if it's okay with you guys? I mean, if you want some privacy, I can—"

"It's your home," Lang said, smiling at her. "We get plenty of privacy. Not to worry."

"Then, home it is," she said, following them to say their good-byes.

As they gathered coats and baby equipment, Robbie caught her in the hall. "Leaving so soon?"

"We're all tired," she said, smiling as she looked into his soft green eyes.

"I can drive you home."

"What about Jane?"

He blushed, waving his arm. "All show. Kyle told me she and Aria have a running bet to see who can attract the most guys."

"Well, I'll leave you to it then."

He took her hand. "What I meant to say is, I'd like to drive you home."

"No, stay. I'll go with Lang and Beth."

"Is everything okay?"

"Fine," she said, gently withdrawing her hand. "Just ready for bed."

"Wish I could be there with you," he whispered, then gazed over, startled to see her expression. "Hope, what's wrong?"

"Nothing. We can talk later." She patted his arm. "Merry Christmas."

"It *is* a merry Christmas, thanks to you." He leaned close and kissed her, more deeply than she expected.

"Hey, you two," Lang said from behind. "Sure you don't want to stay, Hope?"

Face bright red, Hope broke free. "No, all set. Night, Robbie." Before he could say another word, she grabbed the diaper bag and headed out.

"Night, Morgan," she heard Lang say. "Good luck with your redhead."

CHAPTER 43

Tuesday morning, Hope held Lily as Beth packed the diaper bag. Lang was showering after his run before driving Beth and Lily into town for the baby's first checkup.

"We're gonna be late," Beth said, stuffing two tiny rompers into the bag. "I love my husband dearly, but he's never on time."

"Except when it matters," Hope said.

"Oh, so this is how it's going to be, is it? For the next few months, you're going to take his side?"

The remark was said in jest, but Hope could see Beth was on the verge of tears. "Hey, sweetie. You know I'm always on your side."

"I know. Sorry. I guess we'll both be glad to see Haley tomorrow." The therapist had offered to come to the house, but Beth insisted she wanted to get out, so they had made back-to-back appointments.

"Yes," Hope said, patting her arm.

"Have you been avoiding my brother? Haven't seen him since Christmas and he calls constantly. Mother was driving me crazy yesterday so I never got to ask. Everything okay with you two?"

"Yes. No. I don't know. I think it's probably best that we cool it."

"Excuse me?"

"I'm not sure it's the best thing for us to get more involved."

Beth stopped what she was doing and stared at her. "What's going on?"

"Nothing."

"I know my brothers can be jerks."

"It's not that, Beth. Robbie's a great guy."

"And? It's not because of Jane the pain, is it? Because I can tell you, he has absolutely no interest in her. In fact, I've never seen him less interested in anyone than her, or *more* interested in anyone than he is you."

"That's what I'm afraid of."

"What's wrong? Is it too soon after Bruce?"

"No."

"Hope, I don't mean to pry so tell me to back off, but I thought maybe you felt the same way as Robbie?"

"I do."

"Then what's the problem? It's not my overbearing family, is it?"

Hope laughed. "No, I adore your family. You know that. It's kids, Beth."

"I thought you loved kids."

"I do, but I can't...I can't give him any." Her eyes filled as she gazed at her friend.

"Oh, Hopie, if you think he'd care one bit, you're wrong."

"Am I? You see him with Emma, Ben, and Toby. They adore him and he's crazy about them. How can deny him that?"

"One word—adoption."

"But it's not the same, is it?"

"Hey, ladies. Are my two best girls ready to go?" Lang stepped into the kitchen, blond hair mussed and damp. His sky-blue eyes gazed from his wife to Hope, merriment replaced by concern. "Sorry. Am I interrupting?"

Hope smiled at him. "Of course not. You've got two girls who need to get to town."

"Want to come with us?" he asked. "If Beth is up to it, we were going to have lunch at Gracie's after."

"Of course I'm up to it. Yes, do come, Hope! We'd love it."

"This is a family milestone you three should enjoy together."

"There'll be lots more of those ahead. Come. It'll be fun," he said.

"Thanks, but I've got a canvas already set up on the terrace. It's a gorgeous time of day to capture your magnificent view."

"I heard Spark talking with you the other night."

"Yes, he wants me to paint his view. I thought I'd better get back in the saddle. I'm feeling a bit rusty."

"Well, if you're sure?" Beth asked, brown eyes serious.

"Positive. Now scoot or Lily will be late for her first appointment!"

CHAPTER 44

On the glorious Valley morning, Hope had been painting for about an hour when the screen door opened from the kitchen and Beth's dad stepped out, waving.

"Hello, Mr. Morgan!" she called, standing and knocking over the wobbly stool she had found in the barn.

"Hello, darlin', and it's Ben, as you well know." He hugged her warmly. "Just stopped in to see my granddaughter, but doesn't look like they're home."

"No, they're in town. It's Lily's first visit to the doctor. They're probably at Gracie's by now. You might be able to catch them at lunch."

"Much rather sit here in the sunshine talkin' to you. Unless I'd be interrupting?"

"Of course not. Can I get you something to drink?"

"Wouldn't say no to some cold water, if you're sure I'm not bothering you."

Hope smiled at him. "I'll be right back."

She returned, finding him sitting in the shade of the grape arbor. She set two ice waters on a small barrel table and sat beside him. "What a day, huh?"

"A beauty, but then, most Valley days are, even when it rains. You enjoying your stay so far?"

"Very much. I hope I'm helping them."

"You're a godsend. Nora and I are worried about Bethie. She's been so glum. It's good to know you're here to cheer her up."

"We're trying to cheer each other up, sir," she said, then blanched. "I mean…I didn't mean to say. Sorry, that didn't come out right."

He smiled, his wise blue eyes soft. "Valley's a good place to heal."

She nodded. "Yes."

"Wish we could get Robert to stay."

Hope smiled. "I've never heard anyone call him Robert."

He chuckled. "We seldom do, unless he's in big trouble."

"And is he?"

"He's not a happy camper right now, that's for sure."

Hope stared at him for several minutes before speaking. "I'm sorry. Is something wrong?"

"Darlin', you should know that our happiness, Nora's and mine, is completely wrapped up in our kids' happiness. We love them almost as much as we love each other, but if my son has done something to hurt you, I'm sorry."

"Robbie has been nothing but great to me, Mr.…Ben."

"Then can an old man ask why you refuse to talk to him?"

"It's complicated, sir."

"I know you lost someone special to you last year."

"Yes, but that's not it."

As Hope swallowed, wondering what to do, he set down his empty glass. "I'm sorry, sweetheart. I've upset you. I can be a terrible nosey Parker sometimes. I'll let you get back to work."

She reached over to touch his arm as he started to rise. "No, it's okay. I'd like to tell you, if you promise not to say anything to Robbie."

His kind eyes regarded her. "As I said, I'm a nosey Parker, but I'm also discreet. That said, there's no need to say a thing unless you want to."

"I had a procedure last year that left me unable to bear children."

"Oh, darlin', I'm sorry."

"Thank you."

"And you think he would mind?"

"Don't you? He's crazy about children."

He nodded. "He sure loves his niece and nephew."

"He would want children of his own, sir, and I cannot give them to him."

"I think you may be underestimating him."

"Maybe, but I'm not sure I'm strong enough to find out."

"Of course, your decision, darlin'. And your secret's safe with this old man. Won't even tell Nora."

"Thank you."

"Well, gotta get moving and let you get back to work. Heading over to wedding central to see if my buddy's still standing."

Hope smiled, rising to walk him to his truck. "How are the wedding preparations coming?"

"Spark's in his glory and that chef of his has everything well in hand. She's a bit of a martinet, if you ask me. A great cook, but she near drove my wife and Carmela crazy over Christmas dinner."

"He'll be glad to see you, then. Please let them know that I'm happy to help in between my farm and baby duties."

"Will do. You still up at the farm, then?"

"Ruthie called. I promised them the next three days if Beth doesn't need me. After next weekend, she claims she's going back to work, so my babysitting will begin in earnest."

He shook his head, leaning on the hood of his truck. "Too soon. Wish she'd give it a couple more weeks."

"Getting back to work part-time might actually help with the depression," Hope said.

"You might be right. Bye, darlin'. Good luck with that painting. It looks like it's gonna be a beauty. If you're sellin', I'm buyin."

She laughed. "You better wait and see how it turns out first."

"Don't need to. I trust you. Be a great gift for the kids," he said, nodding toward the house.

"My thoughts exactly."

"See ya, darlin'."

"Yes, sir," she said, waving as he headed off.

Hope returned to the terrace feeling more peaceful and happy than she had felt in a long while. It had been good to tell the kind, loving Ben Morgan her secret, even if she could not bear to tell his son.

CHAPTER 45

"Hey, Hope, quittin' time!" Ruthie Morgan called, waving from one of the farm golf carts.

"Should you be driving that?" Hope asked, wiping her brow as she stood up straight.

"Yup. The guys'll be out soon to get those," Ruthie said, indicating the bushel baskets filled with strawberries that lined the row behind her. "You did good, sister. We may have to hire you permanently."

Hope hopped into the cart beside her. "Do you usually do all of this?"

"No way, but Raoul pulled the pickers up to help move the herd today. Robbie's with them. They'll be here tomorrow so you can go back to the herbs. We may need you in the washing shed, too. Did Beth say she'd be okay with the baby?"

"Maybe, if Lang can work from home."

"I know you guys have appointments this afternoon, but have you got time for lunch? My mom had Carmela pack enough for an army, as usual. She's trying to fatten me up after my 'ordeal,' as she calls it."

"It was an ordeal. And thanks, I'd love a quick bite. I have a few minutes cause Martha Dillon's bringing lunch for Beth."

"The invasion of the grandmothers. No wonder Beth wants to go back to work."

Hope watched the youngest Morgan as she hobbled around the farm office, a large basket over one arm. She was quite certain the doctor would not be pleased. "Aren't you supposed to be using crutches?"

"No way. Too cumbersome. Besides, I've always been a fast healer and the leg doesn't hurt a bit," she said, wincing as she stepped down to the porch.

"Not a bit?"

"Well, maybe a little."

"Here, let me take that," Hope said, grabbing the basket. "You sit, and put that leg up, now!"

Baguettes of chicken salad in hand, delicious iced tea at their side, they leaned back, gazing out at the hundreds of acres of farmland.

"Pretty amazing what your family has done here."

"Yup, no place like it on earth. We're lucky. Although right now, I'd like to take a long vacation in Bora Bora."

"How's Kevin doing?"

"Better. He went back to Denver with his folks."

"Oh?"

Ruthie shrugged. "He's called a bunch of times, but I think we're history. The whole thing was too intense for him."

Hope watched her companion, her pale blue eyes staring straight ahead, revealing nothing. Not a classic beauty, Ruthie Morgan was what one would call cute or perky, short and curvaceous, so unlike her slender older sister. Her red curly hair was shoved under a farm baseball cap. The rosiness had returned to her freckled cheeks, but there was a sadness in her expression.

"I'm sorry."

Another shrug. "Wasn't meant to be."

"Does that have anything to do with a certain tall, handsome cowboy?"

"No, it does not! I'm through with Harley Langdon forever, end of story!"

"But he rescued you."

"Humph! I know these mountains better than he does. It was an accident. Could've just as easily happened to Mr. High and Mighty Know-it-all."

"You know that Harley was up for Christmas with Willow when he heard you were missing and practically flew down the highway to help with the search."

"Humph. Still doesn't give him the right to treat me like a baby."

"What happened out there, anyway?"

"Promise you won't tell?" Ruthie asked, staring at her.

"Of course."

"Please, you can't ever tell my brothers or they'll kill him."

"I promise, Ruthie," she said, patting the other's hand.

"I told them Jadie spooked and threw me. That part's true, but I neglected to tell them *why* she spooked. Kevin freaked. Just after we rode under the Dome, a pack of coyotes ran across the trail. They weren't bothering us, just passing through, but Kevin screamed. I reached out my arm to calm him down just as Jadie reared. Before I knew what was happening, I was flying through the air, then tumbling along the rock face. It was a miracle the ledge caught me. I broke my leg hitting it and was knocked out for a short time. When I came to, he was peering over the ledge, screaming and calling to me.

"Later, when I was thinking clearly, I told him to get ropes. He threw the only rope we had down, but it missed me."

"Didn't he have it secured above?"

"He was in a total panic, crying and screaming. He didn't know what he was doing. I told him to throw all the blankets and coats he didn't need down to me and then to ride out to get help. He threw everything down, including his own jacket and what little food and water we had, but refused to move from the edge of the cliff. This lasted for a day and night. Then he disappeared. I never saw him again until you guys hauled me up."

"Oh, Ruthie, that must have been terrible. He was in shock, of course."

She shrugged.

"What a nightmare for you."

"Yup, but it's over and I'm fine. What time's your appointment, anyway?"

"Oh, my goodness!" Hope said, consulting her watch. "Are you okay to clean up?"

"Of course, go. Tomorrow you can tell me why you're not speaking to my poor love-sick brother."

Hope looked back at her. "It's a long story."

"I'm sure, and I'll just bet it's his fault. See ya!"

Hope hurried to the truck, eyes scanning her surroundings in case the brother in question might be in the vicinity.

CHAPTER 46

"Hey, sis," Robbie said, grabbing a water from the office fridge. He had removed his baseball cap and a line of dirt remained on his forehead.

Ruthie nodded. "You're not leavin', are you?"

"I'm sorry, Ruthie. Remember, I promised Dad I'd help out at the Lodge? He's over with Spark doin' God knows what, and Ben's with Harley and the guys at the barn."

"So, you're leaving me? What about Kyle? Why can't he or Sam help at the Lodge?"

"Kyle's still makin' the rounds with Ned, Sam's at the winery, and Rose went to Tucson to meet someone at the clinic. Besides, Raoul and the guys got things covered."

"Well, I sure don't."

"What about Hope? She's out there, isn't she?"

"No, she left to take Beth into town. You just missed her."

"Shit," he muttered.

"What's goin' on with you two?"

"Nothing. Why?"

"Cause you've been mopin' around for three days and she won't talk about it."

"Won't talk to me, either. I've been tryin' to call, but she doesn't pick up."

"What did you do?"

"Nothing. Not a goddamn thing!"

"Well, you certainly let Jane hang all over you. Maybe that drove her away."

"Maybe, but I had the impression she found it funny. She has to know I don't care two hoots about Jane Mackenzie."

Ruthie rolled her eyes. "What do men know, anyway?"

"What's up with you and Langdon?"

"Nothing. He's a jerk."

"He saved your life, sis."

"Did not!"

"Did too."

"And doesn't he know it? Thinks that gives him the right to treat me like a two-year-old. I'm finished with him. I've held on to that crush long enough. Mr. Langdon can go jump in the lake for all I care."

Robbie grinned, watching his sister's face turn red with indignation. She was as crazy about her cowboy as ever. "Hey, gotta go. I'll get here extra early tomorrow and put in a full day, promise."

"Thanks, bro." As he headed for his truck, she called, "And whatever you did to Hope, you better say you're sorry!"

Robbie waved over his shoulder. *Women—there is no figuring them out. One minute I'm sure Hope feels exactly like I do. The next, nothing.*

Chapter 47

Beth took the first appointment with Haley Alverez while Hope held Lily in the therapist's small, light-filled waiting room. Most of the time, the baby slept, but when she woke, her gray-blue eyes studied her caregiver, frowning. When she began to fuss, Hope found a clean diaper, laid out a protective blanket on the wide suede sofa, and changed her. By the time she wrestled the baby back into her onsie, Lily was wailing. Hope scooped her up and began pacing the room, jiggling her up and down. Lily continued to cry, but the wails became whimpers and finally stopped as Hope stood in front of the window, allowing her to gaze out. "Good girl," she whispered. "We don't want to disturb Mommy."

Calm and peace reigned until just before Beth emerged from the inner room. Lily was just beginning to fuss again. Hope gazed up at her friend. "Sorry. Did we disturb you?"

"No, my time's up. Your turn."

"Ready, Hope?" Haley asked, holding the door.

Hope turned to Beth. "You okay?"

"Absolutely. I'm going to feed Lil, then take a short walk. I'll leave the diaper bag but take my phone. Just call if you can't find us. Bye Haley. Thanks so much."

The therapist nodded. "See you next week."

They settled in matching armchairs covered in a soft, mossy-green brocade. Haley looked almost ethereal in jeans and a flowing tunic, her waist-length silver hair falling over her shoulders. She tucked her short legs under her and gave Hope a warm smile. "Would you like tea?"

"No, thanks. I'm fine."

"How're things in the nanny business?"

"Wonderful. I'm so glad to be here."

"I know Beth's grateful for your presence. So, what's happening with you, Hope? How can I help?"

"I hardly know where to begin."

"Well, we can look at today as a beginning. We don't have to cover everything in one hour."

"That's a relief," Hope said, and launched into a brief summary of the past year.

She then recapped her relationship with Robbie since her arrival. "I met him last year, at the wedding, when you and I met. There was an attraction then for sure, at least in my case. I didn't fool myself that he felt the same. In fact, he made it pretty clear that he wasn't interested in anything more than a few dances."

"Are you sure?"

Hope nodded. "Besides, I had a lot of competition. Every woman in the room was after Robbie and his other single brothers. No surprise there. They're all gorgeous."

"They're a handsome lot, I'll give you that. Sounds like things are different this time, though. Sounds like he's very interested."

"That's the problem."

"You're not?"

Hope swallowed, then decided to tell the truth. "I'm hopelessly in love with him, Haley."

"Then, what's the issue?"

"It's not fair to him to get further involved."

"Why?"

"Cause I can't give him what I know he wants."

The therapist's warm gray eyes studied her, but she remained silent, waiting for her to say more.

"Children. I cannot give him children."

"Does he know that?"

"No. Everyone keeps telling me he won't mind and there's always adoption, but you've seen the Morgans. They're an incredibly close family and the kids and grandkids are all clones. They…he would want to carry on the bloodline."

"Hope, I don't know you well and I beg you to forgive me, but that is the biggest load of horseshit I've ever heard."

Hope gazed at the therapist, mouth agape. "I…I…mean, it's…" she said, words trailing off as her eyes filled with tears. "I just don't think I could… I love him and saying good-bye will be hard enough."

"I'm sorry, Hope. I didn't mean to upset you. You've been through so much this past year. Hell and back, really."

Hope sniffed. "It's okay."

"No, it isn't, but I will say is that my comment was not directed at you per se, but more about what I know of the Morgans, from Beth and from observation. I've lived in town for a while and one cannot live in Saguaro Valley and not see a lot of Morgans."

"I'm not sure I understand."

"I'm not sure the bloodlines business fits."

"Maybe not, but I'm not sure I'm strong enough to find out."

"And if you don't, what then?"

"He goes back to Sedona. I stay for a few months as nanny, then head back home."

"Would you be comfortable with that?"

"Time heals."

"But if he's the one and you give him up without fully getting to know him, will you always wonder, do you think?"

Hope shrugged. "I don't know."

"Our time is almost up, but I'd recommend that you weigh those two options—walking away without honesty or telling him and discovering what kind of person Mr. Morgan really is."

"He's a great person and he's been nothing but great to me. I'm pretty sure he'd say it was fine, and talk about adopting and all. I'm just not sure I can do that to him. I know, I know, more horseshit."

"No, but I'd urge you to think about your choices a bit more before turning away. Why not enjoy the week together and see how things go?"

"Because then it will make the turning away even harder."

"Maybe."

"Could we talk again?"

"Of course. Would you like to piggy back on Beth's appointment again?"

"Yes, please."

Haley gave her a card, then hugged her. "Be kind to yourself, Hope."

"Thanks," she said softly, stepping out of the room's warm cocoon. "Will you be at the wedding?"

"Alas, no. I'm spending New Year's with family up north. I hope it's lots of fun."

Hope found Beth and Lily down the street, and they decided to stop in at Gabriela's Dress Shop. The shop owner put up the Closed sign when they entered and played with the baby while they "played," as she called it. Holding Lily, Gabriela whisked around the shop, grabbing "ensembles," clothes that Hope would never have picked out, but which flattered her slender figure and full breasts. As Gabriela rung up Beth's purchases, she begged to pay for Hope's as well, saying, "My husband's filthy rich, you know," but Hope shook her head with a smile. Her pile included two new dresses, shoes, various tops, and a sexy pair of designer jeans. After a gasp of sticker shock, she paid and they were on their way. Gabriela's magic did not come cheap.

CHAPTER 48

Thursday, when Hope drove into the farm lot, Robbie waited, leaning against his truck.

She swallowed hard, grabbed her backpack, and slid out of her truck. "You're up early."

"Only way to catch you, apparently." His smile was warm, eyes wary.

Every inch of her treacherous body ached for him. *Stay strong. Walk by. You can do it, girl.* "Sorry, it's been a crazy few days, and I promised Ruthie I'd start early, so I better get out there."

She attempted to brush by him, but Robbie caught her arm. "Hope, wait! Please."

His touch ignited every fiber of her being. She felt an angry red blush creeping up her neck. It would be so easy to fall into those strong arms. "I'm late. I can't… I've got to get in."

"Ruthie's not even here yet. Please, talk to me. Have I done something to offend you?"

She shook her head, afraid to speak, gazing downward. *If I look into those soft, beautiful eyes, I'm lost.*

"It wasn't Jane, wasn't it?"

"No, of course not."

"Then what? We were getting close, weren't we? What happened?"

"Nothing. I've just been busy, that's all. Beth's needed me and you'll be leaving soon and—"

"Is that it? That I'll be leaving soon? Cause I wanted to talk to you about that."

They turned at the rumble behind them, spying Ruthie drive up in the ranch's antique Ford F1 truck. Her father had restored the old truck many years earlier and then given "my baby to my baby" on Ruthie's eighteenth birthday. She kept it in mint condition, even if a bit dusty most if the time.

"Hey, guys, morning! You two are here early. Thank goodness. We've got a huge day ahead."

Oblivious to the tension in the air, or choosing to ignore it, Ruthie hopped out of the truck and grabbed one crutch from the back.

"Does Dad know you're driving?"

"Yes."

"What about the clutch?"

"Don't worry about me, big brother. It's easy to get from the house to here in second so there's not much shifting. Plus, I've got her trained to my slightest touch. Shifts smooth as silk."

"Well, it won't when you land yourself in a ditch."

"Ha, ha. Why are you standing around? The guys need you. Get moving. Hey, Hope, I'll be inside when you're ready." Ruthie hobbled into the office, leaving them alone again.

"And I thought my brother Ben was a boss," he said, grinning as he scratched his forehead and straightened his baseball cap.

"Well, you heard the boss. I've got to go." She gently extracted herself from his grasp.

"Wait, have dinner with me tonight? Nothing fancy. We can go to the Bulldog."

"There's so much to do with the baby and all. I'm not sure I can get away."

"Please. If you get home and Beth and Lang can't spare you, give me a call. Otherwise I'll pick you up at six thirty. Would that be okay?"

She met his eyes and found them full of sadness and confusion. "Sixty thirty will be fine."

His face lit up with a huge grin. "Great! I'll let you go before you change your mind. See you then."

As he walked away, Robbie Morgan breathed a huge sigh of relief, the scent of sandlewood and orange still lingering from her touch. *Don't know what I've done, but I've got a chance to make it right.*

In jeans and a blue flannel shirt, she looked as lovely as ever, her hair in a braid down her back. The minute she had stepped from the truck, he knew he would do whatever it took to make things right. He had missed her beyond all reason the past few days.

It took several hours of picking and processing herbs before Hope's heart stopped racing and her body settled down from the encounter with Robbie. *How will I ever make it through the evening ahead?*

CHAPTER 49

Beth, Lang, and the baby were at the Dillons' for supper so, wishing to forestall any time alone in the empty house, Hope met Robbie in the driveway. "This outfit okay?" she asked, arms outstretched as he hopped from the truck.

"More than okay. You look sensational, as always." And she did, in one of the light sweaters she had purchased from Gabriela, this one a pale pink, the soft fabric hugging her full breasts.

"Your sister and I went on a bit of a shopping spree."

"I love my sister."

You look pretty sensational yourself, cowboy. Those jeans don't leave much to the imagination, and no one has the right to such a beautiful smile. "It was fun. Shall we?"

All heads turned as they walked into the Bulldog. With its many farms and ranches, the Valley's male population outnumbered the women. Thus, guys were always on the lookout for a pretty face. "I'd better stay close or these wolves'll close in and carry you off," he whispered, hand on the small of her back, as they traversed the dark saloon, its red walls covered with black-and-white rodeo photos, racks of antlers, and a few stuffed heads.

"Hey folks," Russ Keeler called from behind the bar. "What can I get you?"

Robbie turned to her. "What would you like?"

"Actually, after today, I'd love a beer."

"Desert Amber's pretty good."

"Pitcher of DA, Russ, thanks," Robbie said. "And some popcorn or nuts. Anything's fine." He turned to her. "Booth in the back, okay? Hide you away from all these drooling hyenas."

Hope laughed and grabbed the frosted glasses Russ had set on the bar. "I'll save you a seat."

Russ set a full pitcher of beer and a bowl of peanuts on the bar. "Pretty gal, Morgan. No flies on you boys. Have you recovered from the bachelor party?" Keeler referred to Jeb Barnes's small but raucous bachelor party at the saloon several nights earlier.

Robbie grinned. "Just barely. My brothers are wild men."

"You're no slouch yourself. Better get back to your lady. Two of those hyenas are already chatting her up."

"Shit! Thanks, Russ!"

Two twenty-somethings in Saguaro Valley Winery tee shirts stood talking with Hope. Robbie didn't recognize either of them. "Hi, guys," he said, setting down the beer and peanuts. "You new at the vineyard?"

They introduced themselves, Mac and Gene, then shook hands, neither in a hurry to move on. Finally Robbie said, "Well, don't want to keep you, guys. We'll see you around."

Reluctantly, Mac and Gene tipped their hats and headed back to the bar. Hope watched them go, then turned to Robbie. "What were you going to do if they didn't move on?"

He grinned. "Hightail it and take the pitcher with us."

"They seemed nice enough guys. They said they work at the winery."

"Yeah, the Dillons take on a lot of seasonal workers. Not sure what grapes they're harvesting now, though. Thanks for coming tonight. It's really great to see you."

"You, too."

"How have you been?"

"Busy. Lily's found her lungs, and she's especially vocal around two in the morning. Poor Beth's exhausted. Lang and I have been trying to spell her, but she usually insists on getting up."

"She's the food source, right? You and Dad might be fine in the daytime, but I'll bet it's milk she wants in the middle of the night."

"How do you know so much about babies in the middle of the night?"

"I stayed with Ben and Maggie right after Ben the third was born. It was a long two weeks. How's the nursing going?"

"Not so well. Unfortunately, Lily's showing a preference for formula or the ease of delivery with the bottle. Like many new mothers, Beth takes the rejection to heart."

"Still depressed, is she?"

"A little better. Our visit to Haley Alvarez this week helped, I think. It sure helped me."

"You saw her, too?"

Hope nodded. "Good therapists are a gift."

He stared at her, studying her expression. "I guess. Never been to one. Probably should."

"Maybe not. Your life's pretty great and you seem happy and content."

"And you're not?"

"It's a long story."

"Try me."

"Can we order dinner, please? I'm starved."

"Sure. What'd you want? I'll go up and order for us."

They both decided on Bulldog burgers. As he stood, he said, "Looks can be deceiving, you know. I may not be as squared away as I look. No fraternizing while I'm gone, okay?"

Hope smiled. As he turned away, she frowned, wondering what to do. On the one hand, they were just beginning to date, so talking about children seemed ridiculous. On the other hand, she was already in over her head, and the sooner she backed away, the less heartache she would face. Maybe him, too.

He returned and caught her unawares, perplexed by the sadness he glimpsed even as she forced a smile. "What's wrong, Hope? You can tell me."

"It's a lot of things."

"Still mourning your friend?"

"Yes."

"Did we move too fast?"

"No…yes…I don't know. It's not that, or Bruce, really."

"I'm a good listener," he said, reaching over to take her hand. "And I hope you know I'm a friend."

Hope swallowed, looking up to find such warmth in his gaze. "The thing is, Robbie, I really like you. This past week has been amazing."

"Ditto. I really like you, too."

"But the thing is, I more than like you. I'm falling in love with you."

"And that's a problem, why?"

"Because there's so much that you don't know about me."

"I know you're an incredible woman and a good friend to a sister I love very much. Christ, you've put your own life on hold to come help Beth."

"Maybe I need her more than she needs me? Truth is, I had to get away from Tintown and from my life."

"Well, you landed in a perfect getaway spot surrounded by people who care about you and are thrilled that you're here. Lang said the other day that he wished you'd stay on for a year or two."

"He says that now."

"He meant it. Morgans, and Dillons who've now been Morganized, are never as happy as when their houses are full."

"Well, I'm very lucky, then." Her long, slender fingers stroked his rough, callused palm. *Such strength in every inch of him.*

"You know if you keep that up much longer, I'm gonna get a hard-on and won't be able to walk out of here."

She grinned, gazing up as Russ Keeler approached, carrying two platters of food. "Oh, my goodness, it will take three weeks to eat all that!"

Each plate was piled high with curly fries, coleslaw, and the most enormous burgers she had ever seen. "We've got takeout boxes," Russ said. "Give a wave and I'll bring some over later. Enjoy."

She groaned, biting into the thick, juicy burger. The menu had extolled the virtues of locally grown food and she had to agree. More than likely this was the Dillons' prize angus beef, with the potatoes and vegetables grown at Morgan's Run. "This is incredible."

"Nothin' like it," he said, tipping his burger in her direction. "Nothin' like you, either."

They ate in silence, then sat back, enjoying satiety and one another's company. He didn't ask to resume their previous conversation and Hope decided to let it be. Instead, she asked him to tell her more about life in Sedona. Finally he waved to Russ, who brought the check. "My treat," he said as Hope reached for her purse. Money on the table, he looked up, meeting her eyes. "Can I take you someplace else? It's kind of a favorite spot of mine."

"Does it involve hiking? I need to walk off this dinner."

"Not much, but let's see how things go. A walk is certainly a possibility."

"Remembering that we rise before the sun?" she asked, her legs wobbly. Two beers had left her light-headed and tipsy.

"Come on. Let's run the gauntlet," he said, taking her hand. "Feel free to lean on me, babe."

CHAPTER 50

"Here we are," he said, turning in to a dirt road just before the hill leading up to the farm office. He drove a short distance and parked the truck. "Short hike from here so you got your wish."

"Where are we?"

"You'll see. Come on." He took her hand and led her up the road. After a short walk, they came into a clearing, the silhouette of a tiny structure outlined in the moonlight at the crest of the hill. "Welcome to the Dobby House."

"What is it?"

In answer, he led her up onto a small porch, then reached up with his left hand, feeling above the doorjamb. "Here we go."

Robbie opened the door and reached round for a light switch. When the light came on, Hope could not have been more surprised if the Easter Bunny appeared. They stood in a tidy wood-paneled room, the walls lined with photos. To the left, a counter held a sink, hot plate, tea kettle, and a few other items. A shelf above held odd pieces of pottery and a basket of cutlery. Below the counter was a small fridge. On the opposite wall was a fireplace, two chairs on either side. Straight ahead stood a rough-hewn four-poster bed covered with a brightly colored patchwork quilt and plump pillows covered in white eyelet.

"What is this place?"

"A gift from my dad to our mom on their tenth wedding anniversary. It's their place, where they go to get away, just the two of them. It was just an old shack when Dad and Raoul spent months restoring it. Pretty cool, huh?"

"Very cool and private. I feel like we're intruding."

"It's fine. I asked Dad."

"You what!" Hope blushed crimson. "I can't believe you—"

"Hold your horses. Calm down. I asked if we could come here for a cup of tea and a quiet place to talk. That's all."

"Yeah, right, and he believed you?"

"Who cares? He said yes so here we are. Want a fire? Some tea?"

"So now your dad's colluding to get me into your bed, too!"

Robbie grinned, moving to the hearth and grabbing matches from the mantle. The dry kindling flamed instantly. "Well, if that's what you want, we can skip the tea."

"Ha, ha." Hope crossed her arms, gazing around at the beautiful space, not sure whether to be embarrassed, angry, or grateful.

"Hey," he said, crossing the room and touching her arm. "If this makes you uncomfortable, we can go."

Hope met his eyes. *I can trust this man.* She reached up, arms circling his neck and drew him closer. Every fiber of her body ached for his touch, his kiss. *One last time won't hurt, and I'm going to miss him so much.* Her lips found his and she kissed him, her tongue teasing, stroking, and delving deeper.

Without a word, he lifted her, wrapping her legs around his waist and carrying her to the bed. "Am I reading the signals right?"

Hope nodded. "If you think this is okay? Using the bed, I mean?"

In answer, Robbie laid her down and gently unbuttoned her jeans, slipping them off along with her boots and socks. He stroked her belly, hands slowly lifting her tee shirt, moving to the bottom edge of her lacy white bra. "Beautiful," he murmured, slipping the shirt over her head and trailing kisses from her neck to the sweet valley between her glorious breasts. He cupped both breasts, fingers teasing the lace round her nipples until they hardened, and Hope moaned softly.

"You like?" he asked, slipping the bra off.

"What do you think?" she whispered. "But I cannot help but notice you're still fully dressed." As she spoke, her fingers stroked the erection that strained at his jeans. Its size took her breath away. Slowly she began unbuttoning him, stroking and rubbing his penis as she worked.

"Sweetheart, you're killing me," he said, voice gruff. "Not sure how long I can hold on."

He leaned over to kiss her.

"Oh, no, my turn," she said, releasing him as she moved closer, taking him in, her wet lips sliding his length, tongue stroking, teasing, circling.

"Oh, my God," he cried, grabbing the bedpost to steady himself.

Hope withdrew for an instant, gazing up at him. "Why don't you lie down beside me, cowboy? Wouldn't want you to topple over."

She patted the bed and he slipped down, attempting to take her in his arms. "What did I say, Mr. Morgan? This is my turn."

As she straddled him, Robbie marveled at her glorious body, breasts full, round, and perfect, flat, muscular belly and slim, smooth hips, her white lacy panties still in place. He tried to reach down, to caress her, but Hope held him back, bending over to take him in her mouth once again, this time falling into a smooth, agonizing rhythm that carried him to heights he'd never climbed before. "Oh, God, oh, God, oh, God" heralded his last seconds of coherence as he lost himself in a crashing, thunderous ejaculation.

Overcome with the intensity of his release, and her part in bringing it on, Hope smiled, resting her head on his strong thigh, trying to catch her breath. As she lay still, her fingers trailed up and down his calf. She had never experienced anything like this. Never been with a man who experienced such a powerful, earthshaking orgasm. She had been as aroused as he and was almost afraid to meet his gaze.

After a few minutes, he reached down and began stroking her hair. "Hey," he said softly. "Come here, will you?"

Slowly she inched up until she lay in his arms. Only then did she dare meet his eyes. What she found was warmth, gratitude, and love. "You okay?" she whispered.

"Thank you," he said, pulling her close and kissing her deeply. "That was the most incredible moment of my life."

"I'm glad," she said, smiling at him. "Even though I'm sure you'll think of some others when you're saner."

"I doubt it," he said, kissing her nose. "You know what this means, of course?"

Hope grinned, a mischievous twinkle in her eyes. "No, do tell."

"My turn," he whispered, trailing kisses from her lips down her neck. Hope attempted to follow suit, but he settled her hands at her side, taking one and then the other breast, tongue teasing, tickling, and sending Hope into oblivion. He then moved down to her belly, gently spreading her smooth, soft thighs as his fingers slipped between them to plumb her wet, warm depths. He lifted his head, smiling at her. "Someone else got pretty excited back there. Let's see if there's more to come."

As tongue replaced fingers and Robbie thrust, stroked, and delved deeper, Hope cried, "No, no, no!" lost in a sea of sensation. Her orgasm came in a blaze of white light as he held her hips in his strong hands. She struggled to catch her breath as he began kissing her inner thighs, moving lower to her knees, calves, and feet, teasing, tickling, and prompting sensations she had never known before. "Oh, oh," she whispered as his lips began their slow ascent back up her thighs, tongue once again parting her labia, finding her sweet spot.

As he moved, she gazed down, realizing that he was fully erect, yet she could not reach him. So wet, Hope was sure buckets were pouring out of her, but certain she would die if she did not have the thing she craved. "Robbie Morgan, I want you inside of me now. Please!" It was her last moment of clarity before she felt the full force of his presence, filling her, completing her, sending her sky high in a flame of ecstasy.

They matched each other's moves in a slow, rapturous dance of passion and ultimately frenzy. Each could not get enough of the other. Their perfect symmetry rose to a blinding, joyful climax, leaving them spent and blissfully sated.

"I love you," he whispered as they lay in each other's arms.

Hope wanted to return his words, telling him that she loved him beyond all reason and thought, but she stayed silent, kissing his hard, strong chest in reply, still filled and at home with him inside her as they drifted off to sleep.

CHAPTER 51

An hour later, Hope woke to his kiss on her forehead. "Hey, sweetheart, it's getting late. Much as I'd like nothing better than to spend the night here with you, that's against the Dobby House rules."

"And we both have to be up early," she said, snuggling closer, reveling in his touch and the strong arms enfolding her.

As he withdrew, Robbie groaned. It felt as if he had lost his heart, his center, his home. No woman had ever been able to fully take him, hold him, accept his fully erect penis, and most had had to pull away in pain. The realization that this incredible wozman could welcome him so fully and completely was a miracle. "How 'bout some tea before we go?"

"Sounds lovely."

He kissed her, then rose. "Those chairs by the fire are pretty comfy."

"So, you've done this before."

His face fell, and she realized her flippancy had been misguided. "By myself. It used to be my getaway place. I think we've all used it at one time or other, but we're respectful of it and what it means to Mom and Dad."

"They're quite a couple, aren't they?"

"Hard act to follow. They're still crazy about each other even after nearly forty years."

"Your brothers and sisters seem to have done pretty well in that department."

"Ceylon or Earl Gray?"

"You choose. I love both."

"Yeah, Ben, Beth, and Sam are pretty happy, but Ben and Mags have had some rough patches. Sam and Rose, too. I don't think my parents have had so much as a rough day, hour, or minute."

"You never know, but you're probably right. They seem like such a love couple."

Robbie laughed. "Thanks to Dad. He's definitely the peacekeeper. Here you go." He handed her a steaming mug of Earl Gray.

"So, here we are. I'm a good listener, or we can just enjoy the fire," he said, reaching over to take her hand. "After what you just gave me, I owe you big-time."

"You don't owe me anything. Words could never say," she said, stroking his palm, her blue eyes liquid as she met his. "I'm not even sure where we left off. Maybe it's not the right time."

"Your choice, Hope. I won't press you," he said, leaning back, releasing her hand.

She swallowed. *Now or never, I guess.* "It's been a rough year, but my reticence now is fear of getting closer."

"Don't think two people can get much closer than we just were, sweetheart. Remind me why getting closer is a problem?" His beautiful eyes watched her, puzzled but kind.

"Because saying good-bye will be much harder later."

"Why the hell would we be saying good-bye?"

"Let's face it. You'll be heading back to Sedona next week, Robbie. We live and work in different worlds."

"I can't speak for you, but I'm not planning to live in Sedona forever. It's great, but it's not home." To his surprise, tears began to trickle down her beautiful cheeks. "Hope, what have I said?"

"It's not you. It's me. I mean, we hardly know each other and I'm already thinking about a future that will probably never happen."

"Foolish me, I'd like to think we had a future."

"As friends?"

"Babe, what we just shared was a lot more than I've shared with friends. Ever."

"Yes," she said, smiling through the tears.

"Then what's the issue?"

"I know you know about Bruce's death, but what I haven't told you is that I was pregnant last year. The baby was his. I made a decision, a very painful decision. I'm not sure it was the right one, but it's done."

"Did you find out about the family?"

"I'm sorry? What family?"

"The ones who took the child? That must have been hell to give him or her up."

She shook her head, wondering if she could or should say any more. Finally she swallowed hard. "You misunderstand. I had an abortion, Robbie."

"Oh, God, that must have been tough."

"It was."

"Was Bruce with you?"

"No, he didn't know about it until after it happened. There were complications. I had a post-procedure infection and a lot of bleeding. I almost died. Would have died if Bruce hadn't found me and gotten me to the hospital."

"Oh, sweetheart, I'm so sorry."

She nodded. "Bruce stayed with me the whole time even though he knew what I'd done and his heart was breaking over the baby. His family are devout Catholics."

"How soon after that did he die?"

"Two months. I'm convinced he took the undercover assignment because of what I'd done and the death of his child."

Her shoulders shook with sobs and Robbie knelt in front of her, arms enfolding her. "Poor baby, you can't know that."

"But I do."

"Well, it's over now and you're safe. I've got you, sweetheart."

"That's just the trouble," she sobbed. "I mean, you're not a problem, but it would be if we became more involved."

He reached up, gently wiping tears away. "You lost me there, babe."

"The abortion, it left me…I can't bear children, Robbie."

"Oh, Hope, I'm so sorry," he said, drawing her down to sit on his lap, folding her into his arms.

He held her until her sobs subsided. The fire was almost out and the cabin had grown cold. "Hey," he said softly. "You ready to head back?"

Hope nodded as she pulled away from his warmth and stood. Robbie scattered the remains of the embers, making sure the fire was out as she washed the tea mugs and set them back on the shelf. They worked together, straightening the bed, changing the sheets, smoothing the quilt, and fluffing the pillows. As she pulled on her sweater against the chill, he placed his hands on her waist, meeting her eyes. "You okay?"

She nodded.

"We better head out." He kissed her lightly, then opened the door.

Neither spoke on the short drive to Lang and Beth's. When he stopped the truck, she leaned over and kissed his cheek. "Don't get out. It's late. See you tomorrow."

Before Robbie could respond, she was halfway up the walk. He watched her step inside and close the door, then drove off. He couldn't deny that Hope's news had shocked him to the core, but he also could not deny his powerful feelings for her. He decided that the best thing to do was give it a few days. *Too late to think about this tonight.*

Hope closed the front door and leaned against it in the quiet of the house. They had left a light on for her, but no one stirred. "I'm so sorry," he had said, but nothing else. *Robbie Morgan is already pulling back as I knew he would and should. Only this weekend to get through. Then the process of mending yet another broken heart can begin.*

CHAPTER 52

Jeb Barnes's parents were hosting a rehearsal dinner at the Lodge, where they were staying. Spark and Amy's Portland friends were also in residence at the ranch's luxurious inn. Hope put in a half day at the farm, then came home to babysit so that Beth could help out at the Lodge. Maggie swung by to pick up Beth around one, and they went off giggling like two schoolgirls. Her friend continued to struggle with depression, and Hope prayed that the afternoon off would lift her spirits.

Robbie had not called, and she dreaded seeing him that evening. She had offered to babysit so Lang and Beth could enjoy the dinner, but Martha Dillon had insisted on coming. "Tonight is for carefree young people," Lang's mother had told her. "You go have fun, honey. I'm happy to sit with my precious granddaughter for a few hours."

Carefree—that's a laugh, Hope thought, settling the sleeping baby in her portable crib in the kitchen while she washed lunch dishes. *I wonder if I'll ever feel carefree again.*

*****

Robbie and Ruthie worked a full day at the farm, then headed home to shower. They drove up to the big house at the same time and found their parents on the porch, enjoying the warm afternoon. "Hey, you two," Leonora said. "Come join us for a drink. Plenty of time before the shindig."

"I'm surprised you aren't up there supervising," Ruthie said, hobbling up the steps and plunking clumsily into a porch rocker.

"Jim Thompson and his staff have everything well in hand, young lady," she said, referring to the Lodge manager. "And where are your crutches?"

Her daughter rolled her eyes, then winked at her father. "What about you, Dad? I should think you'd wanta be in on the action?"

"Your brothers are up there. That's enough."

He looks tired, Robbie thought, wondering if something was wrong. "You okay, Dad?"

"Never better. My Nora wanted me to keep her company and she's very persuasive." He reached over and patted her hand. "'Sides, this is the Barnes's night. They don't need an old geezer interfering with their arrangements. Jeb's sisters, Lesley and Catie, have the whole thing planned. The Lodge staff assures me that the Barnes sisters are expert party planners."

Robbie nodded at Carmela, who had appeared with a beer for him and lemonade for Ruthie. "Has the wedding party taken over the whole place?" he asked.

"There are two rooms with non-wedding guests," Ben Senior said, "but Jim's arranged an evening in Tucson for them. Dinner, music, dancing. Mel and Rita closed the Spa for the night and are driving them down." Jim Thompson had been with the ranch as assistant manager, then manager for almost two decades. His staff adored him and he had trained them well. Mel Farrell and her partner, Rita Lazares, had run the ranch's state-of-the-art Spa and workout studios for over ten years.

Leonora turned to her son. "So sweetheart, how did your evening with Hope go?"

"Very late!" Ruthie said. "He's been dragging around all day. Surprised he didn't fall asleep on the tractor."

"Hush, Ruthie Ann. I was addressing your brother."

"Fine, Mom. We had a nice time."

"Doesn't look like it from your expression, sweetie."

His father exchanged looks with Ruthie, then turned to Robbie, eyes thoughtful. "Where'd you eat?"

"Bulldog. Every man in the place had his tongue hangin' on the floor. They need to import some more women to this Valley." His joking was meant to deflect his mother, who honed in on trouble like a hawk eying its prey.

Ruthie decided a change of subject was in order. "Have you seen Buck Foster yet?" She referred to Amy's brother and Spark's son, a successful artist who lived in Laguna Beach, with whom Ruthie had flirted shamelessly during his last visit.

"Nope, but I hear he's arrived," Ben Senior said.

"Can't wait. He and Hope would have a lot in common. I can't remember. Have they met?" Ruthie grinned at all three of them. *I'll just bet Hope told my dumb brother her secret and he reacted like a jerk. A little competition won't hurt.*

"Ruthie Ann, don't be ridiculous!" Leonora said. "The things you come up with. What are you wearing tonight, anyway? That cast is going to present a problem."

Robbie stood, setting his empty bottle on the table. "That's my cue. If you ladies are going to talk fashion, I'm heading for the shower."

CHAPTER 53

Hope dressed carefully for the evening's event, choosing one of the dresses she had purchased at Gabriela's. This one, a linen sheath in a deep red shade, fit her snugly, flattering her slender frame and full breasts. The neckline plunged, revealing a hint of cleavage, and the short skirt accentuated her long, slim legs. She slipped on a pair of strappy black sandals and a gold necklace and matching earrings. Ordinarily she favored silver, but Gabriela had convinced her that this particular set would complement the dress perfectly. As Hope gazed in the bathroom's full-length mirror, she had to admit that the dress and jewelry worked. She applied mascara and lipstick, then swept her hair back, holding it in place with two gold combs, also recommended by Gabriela. *Robbie has never seen my hair down*, she mused as she heard a knock at the door.

It was Lang, looking dapper in a blue sport jacket and khakis. "Wow!" he said, eying her from head to toe. "What happened to our nanny? You look spectacular, Hope."

"Especially compared to your frumpy wife?" Beth asked, coming up behind him, Lily in her arms. She wore an understated beige linen dress, her hair falling round her shoulders.

Lang turned and whistled. "You look more beautiful tonight than I've ever seen you, darling." His gaze, so full of love and affection, brought a smile to his wife's face. The doorbell rang. "That will be Grandma," he added, taking the baby from Beth and heading downstairs.

"You are so lucky," Hope said. "You have the best husband in the world."

"He's pretty great, isn't he? You do look terrific, by the way. Gabby was sure right. That dress is made for you."

Hope laughed. "Gabriela the miracle worker."

"You okay?" Beth asked, meeting her eyes. "You've been kind of subdued since your dinner with Robbie. Did things go alright?"

"It was fine."

"Why don't I believe you?"

"I told him the whole story and he was very kind and supportive, until he heard about my barrenness."

"Oh, Hope, what did that lummox say?"

"That he was very sorry for me. He was okay, but it was obvious he was totally freaked out and trying to hide it."

"Are you sure?"

"Come on, ladies! Time to go," Lang called.

"We can talk later," Hope said. "I'm be fine, really."

Chapter 54

Jeb's parents and siblings greeted them in the lobby of the Lodge, the bride and groom a short distance away, talking to friends. A handsome, sandy-haired man, with striking blue eyes and broad shoulders stood next to Spark Foster, chatting to a couple Hope had never seen. *Buck Foster, I presume. Pretty cute, too.*

"Good evenin', folks!" Spark called, waving as he spotted them. "This is Beth Morgan and her husband Lang. You remember them, don't you, Buck?"

"Of course," he said, extending his hand.

"Hi, Buck, great to see you," Beth said. "This is my dear friend, nanny, and houseguest, Hope Seymour. I can't remember. Have you two met before?"

"I don't think so. Hello," Hope said, extending her hand.

As he gave her a firm handshake, Buck grinned. "The lady in red. I remember you from the wedding, but we were never introduced. Nice to finally meet one of the Southwest's most gifted artists."

Hope blushed. "I don't know about that, but good to meet you."

"Can I buy you a drink, Ms. Seymour?"

"Buck's kidding of course. No charge tonight," Spark said, clapping his son on the back.

"I'd love red wine, Mr. Foster, and it's Hope, please."

"Come on then," he said, touching the small of her back as he guided her toward the bar.

At that moment, Robbie walked in with his parents, Ruthie, and Kyle, and spied the cozy couple.

Ruthie clapped her hands. "See, what'd I tell you? Buck and Hope have already hooked up."

Kyle whistled. "Wow, she sure doesn't look like a nanny tonight."

Robbie glared at his brother and sister before turning away to greet the Barnes family and Amy and Jeb. He had noted every inch of his lover as she turned and waltzed off with Buck Foster. His heart and body ached for her touch, even if his warring emotions held him back.

"Hey, buddy," his brother Ben said, clapping his shoulder. Harley and Nick Parker were with him, beers in hand. "You look like you just lost your best friend."

"Looks more like lovesickness to me," Harley said, grinning.

"Ha, ha. Lay off, guys. I'm not in the mood," Robbie said, stalking off.

"What's with him?" Ben said to no one in particular.

"Who?" Maggie asked, coming up from behind.

"My brother."

"Trouble in Paradise," Harley said. "The beautiful nanny has found a fellow artist and they look pretty chummy."

"What have I missed?" Ben asked, eying his best friend.

"Everything," Maggie said, laughing as she hugged him. "That's why I love you so much."

Sam Morgan and Rose Dillon met Robbie at the bar. "Evenin', brother. How goes it?"

"Great. How 'bout you two? I've barely seen you this visit."

Sam nodded. "It's been hectic. Let's at least catch breakfast or lunch before you leave."

"When is that?" Rose asked.

"I'm supposed to head back Monday, but they're pushing me to come back Sunday. We've got a lot of tours booked and I'm leaving them short-staffed."

"I should think this'd be their slow season," Sam said, watching his brother watch Hope Seymour.

Robbie tore his eyes away from Hope and shook his head. "Not this year. It's been the darndest thing. We usually start to kick back right after Labor Day, but things haven't letup yet. We keep waiting for the lull, but we're still getting bookings left and right."

Rose smiled. "That's a good thing, right?"

"Depends on how you look at it."

She looked across the foyer and spied Hope for the first time. "Doesn't Hope look lovely tonight? I'll just bet she got that dress at Gabriela's."

"Don't know where she got it," Sam said, "but it's a keeper. I thought you guys had a thing, bro. What's she doing with Buck Foster?"

"Fellow artists," Robbie said as dinner was announced.

The tables held place cards, and Hope found hers next to Lang's and Beth's, her friend on her right and Robbie on her left. He was nowhere to be seen when she sat down, but soon appeared, full beer in hand. "Hey," he said, slipping in beside her.

"Hello," she said softly.

"You look amazing, by the way."

"You, too," she said, forcing a smile. And he did look amazing in a beige linen sport coat and pale blue shirt, his scent of citrus and musk intoxicating.

"Your friend Foster certainly noticed."

He was not entirely successful in keeping sarcasm from his tone, and Hope stiffened. Thankfully, the dinner conversation and numerous toasts made conversation unnecessary through most of the meal. Amy and Jeb looked so happy. She was a beautiful woman inside and out, and he clearly adored her. Their son, Toby, was at the Big House with Emma and baby Ben. Their shared love of him had only increased the depth of their feelings for one another. *Another lucky couple,* Hope thought, watching them.

As everyone mingled after dinner, Beth found Hope talking to Spark and his son. "Hey, Hope, I'm beat. Lang and I are going to head out. You don't have to come. Stay. I know someone will bring you home."

"I'd be happy to," Buck said.

"Thanks, but I'm pretty beat myself. I'll just say good-bye to Amy, Jeb, and his family. It was a lovely party, Spark. See you tomorrow."

"And I'll see you in the morning, right?" Buck asked. "Nine o'clock at the barn? I spoke to Harley and he'll have the guys saddle up the horses."

"That is, if Beth can spare me," Hope said, turning to her friend.

"My fault," Buck said. "I made Hope promise to take a short ride with this city slicker. Langdon promised to give me the gentlest horse."

"Of course we can spare you. Good night, Spark, Buck. See you at the wedding."

As Beth and Hope headed over to say their good-byes, Robbie intercepted them. "Hey, I've been looking for you." He gently took hold of her arm.

Beth left them alone and Hope turned to him. "We're just saying our good-byes."

"Let me take you home."

"Thanks, but I'm all set with Beth and Lang."

"But I want to, Hope. There are things to be said."

"Not tonight," she said, gently easing herself from his grasp. *Not ever.* "Good night."

As he watched her walk away, Robbie felt like his heart had been ripped from his chest. Still, he stayed rooted to the spot, until two young women from Portland sidled up to say hello.

CHAPTER 55

"Thanks for taking it slow," Buck said as they rode side by side on the ranch's wide Loop Trail. Nick had saddled Tara for him, and so far he had managed to stay in the saddle.

"No problem," Hope said. "It's a beautiful morning, and where else in the world do you get views like this?"

"Oh, I don't know. The Pacific is pretty spectacular."

She laughed. "Well, that's true."

"If you don't mind my asking, how is it that a beautiful woman like you isn't with someone?"

Hope looked over, wondering at the question. *Why do people always assume women need men to complete them?*

Noticing her expression, he said, "Sorry. Dumb question."

"Kind of, but that's okay." She realized she felt at ease with Spark's son, not cornered and not even attracted to him, although Buck was handsome and sexy.

"There is someone, isn't there?"

"Yes."

"One of those unattached Morgans, I'll wager?"

"Ready for a canter?" she asked, nudging Whimsy into the wide-open meadow. The horse took off at a gallop instead, and Tara followed suit.

"Aah! Stop!" he called, hanging on for dear life.

Fearing for his safety, she reined up and waited, but Tara did not stop. She shot past, headed for the far side of the meadow. "Shit, hold on," she cried, taking off after them.

As she neared Tara, Hope leaned to the right, arm outstretched, managing to grab the slack reins that Buck had let go.

"Whoa, girl, hey," she said as the frightened horse slowed and finally stopped.

"What the hell are you doing?" a voice called from the south, and she turned in time to see Robbie approaching. "You could have killed him and yourself!"

Buck was slumped over, still holding Tara's mane in a death grip. "No problem, Morgan. I'm fine."

"And so am I, thank you," Hope said. "What're you doing out here, anyway?"

"Checking fences. Some of the cattle are missing." This was true, but he had volunteered for the job this morning after learning that Hope had gone riding with Buck Foster.

"They aren't even grazing here."

"Next week. You okay, Foster?"

"Ducky," the other man said, gazing from Robbie to Hope. He had clearly discovered the object of Hope's affection. The connection between the two was electric. Buck had a live-in girlfriend and wasn't looking for love. Only a diversion for wedding weekend. *Maybe best to stay out of this threesome?*

Furious and embarrassed, Hope said, "Come on, Buck. We better head back."

"You're sure you're okay?" Robbie said to no one in particular.

"Fine!" she said a trifle too sharply.

Buck grinned, watching the interplay. "Never better. Thanks, man." He sat up, taking hold of the reins as Tara followed Whimsy at a slow trot.

"I'm really sorry," Hope said as they neared the stables. "That was incredibly stupid of me."

"No harm done," Buck said. "Now I know the answer to my question, though."

"It's complicated."

But hot. "Looks like it. Think you'll work it out?"

She shrugged. "Not likely, but thanks for asking. What about you? Is there someone special?"

"I live with someone. Her name's Kelly."

"Why isn't she here?"

"She's a musician and she had a gig."

"I'm surprised your dad and Amy didn't tap her for the wedding."

"My dad and Kelly don't get along."

"Oh? I thought Spark got along with everyone."

"Let's just say they don't see eye to eye on any subject you can name, and they're both stubborn as hell."

Nick Parker approached. "I'll take 'em in," he said, grabbing the reins of both horses.

"Are you sure, Nick? I can stay and cool her down," she said.

"No prob. We're pretty slow this morning and the stalls are all set. They're going out for the day after a brush down."

"Thanks," she said, smiling at the handsome wrangler. "Horse whisperer," they called him, and he was amazing with all animals.

"See you at the wedding," he said as they headed into the barn.

Buck walked Hope to her truck. "Thanks. Great way to wake up."

"I'm sorry, Buck."

"Don't be. It was fun. No broken bones. Maybe a little bruised pride. I won't be auditioning for *Horsemen of the Apocalypse* anytime soon."

She smiled. "It's amazing what a little practice will do."

"And good luck with Morgan. You two have something going on. That's obvious. I hope it works out for you."

"Maybe," she said, hopping into the truck. "See you in a few hours."

CHAPTER 56

Amy and Jeb were married in Spark's backyard under an arbor covered with desert flowers and greenery. Over three acres of lawn stretched in front of the assemblage, new sod planted two weeks earlier, but appearing to have been there forever. Harley was best man, and Jessie, a friend of Amy's from Portland, was maid of honor. Harley carried Toby, the ring bearer, down the aisle and they shared duties in that department. The handsome wrangler held the child throughout the ceremony.

Harley's daughter, Willow, sat with Nick Parker and Ben, Maggie, and family. Fifteen now, Willow was growing into a beautiful young woman, her long, flaxen hair tied with a pale green bow that matched her simple dress. The color suited her. Hope sat with Beth and Lang, next to his parents and Rose and Sam. At one point, he turned and looked back, catching her eye, but she quickly looked away.

Hope checked the reception seating, finding that she and Robbie were not at the same dinner table. She didn't know whether to be glad, relieved, or sad. She managed to avoid him during the cocktail hour by gluing herself first to Jeb's sisters, who were both warm and friendly, then to Buck Foster, who was only too happy to be rescued from Ruthie's attentions. It was clear Ruthie was flirting with any man she could find.

Buck nodded as Hope came to stand beside him, the two of them observing the youngest Morgan fling herself at Nick Parker. "That cast doesn't seem to be slowing Ruthie down, does it?"

Hope laughed. "I believe this is for the benefit of a certain handsome cowboy."

"Haven't they been doing this dance for several years?"

"So I understand."

"And Dad told me the guy saved her life. What's with her?"

"Well, she's a redhead, for one. I also think Harley's a bit elusive. It's clear he loves her, but maybe isn't ready to settle down? Who knows. The scuttlebutt has always been that he thinks she's too young for him, but he kind of blew his cover on that one when she went missing."

"Hard to know with affairs of the heart, isn't it? Where's your cowboy tonight?"

"He's around," she said, eyes scanning the crowd but failing to spot him.

"Haven't made up, then?"

"Can we please talk about something else?"

*****

Aria grabbed Robbie and Kyle to help move some cases of wine and beer. When they re-entered the tent, he frowned, spying Hope with Buck Foster. She looked ethereal in a pale pink sleeveless dress, a glittery shawl draped round her shoulders and sparkling silver at her neck. *The most beautiful woman in the world and there she stands with Buck Foster again. What's with that guy? Doesn't he know anyone else?*

"What's wrong, bro?" Kyle asked. "You look ready to kill."

He shrugged. "It's nothing. Let's get a beer."

Aria and her catering staff put on a sumptuous feast, every course grander and more exquisite than the previous one. Wait staff passed everything from luscious salads to fish, chicken, pork, and beef, all ingredients local. The dessert platters followed with ice cream cups, crème brûlée, mousse, pies, and cookies. Neither Jeb nor Amy liked cake, but the bakery in town had made a small cake in the shape of a javelina, which the bride and groom cut with Toby's help. The children were seated at a small table next to the bride and groom's table. Ruthie had volunteered to sit with the three and keep order. Emma and Toby were good as gold, but she had her hands full with Ben the third, who rarely sat anywhere for more than three minutes.

After excusing herself from Buck Foster, Hope came to sit with Beth and Lang, the three watching as Ben and Maggie's youngest crawled under the table, with his aunt, face beet red, following suit.

"Poor Ruthie," Beth said. "I told Maggie baby Ben could stay with Lily. I'm sure Martha and Neecy could handle him for a few hours." She referred to Lang's mother and the Dillon's housekeeper, Neecy Rodriquez. Hope smiled. "He is a handful. I'm still feeling guilty that Martha had to miss the wedding."

"Believe me, she's where she wants to be. She doesn't know Amy and Jeb that well, Lang's dad is in one of his funks, and she loves spending time with Lily. Anything to get away from Jaybo for a few hours."

"It's tough for her, isn't it?"

Beth leaned closer, whispering. "Jaybo Dillon is a bastard. He was a bastard before he was sick and now he's worse. We were all afraid of him as kids. The alcoholic's moods are so unpredictable. We never knew when he'd been drinking and Jaybo is a mean drunk."

"Must be so hard on Lang."

"Why do you think he moved to Boston? For years, poor Rose had to shoulder the burden, but thankfully she's escaped. With Rose and Sam in Maryland, Lang feels it's his turn to take over for a while. He handles it, but there's a lot of anger there. I've tried to get him to see Haley, but he refuses."

Lang leaned over, arm around Beth. "Hey, ladies, how're you doin'?"

Beth leaned into his shoulder. "Perfect, sweetheart."

Hope watched the two, so loving and generous with each other. She suspected Lang had overheard their conversation, but she saw nothing but affection in his gaze.

"So, Hope," he said. "When are you gonna put my pathetic brother-in-law out of his misery?"

"Excuse me?"

"Lang, leave her alone."

Lang shrugged, blue eyes dancing with mischief. "Okay, but our Robbie's been mopin' around like a sick puppy."

"Stop it!" Beth said, poking him. "And if he has, he deserves it."

As husband and wife bantered back and forth, Hope scanned the tent, spying Robbie two tables over between Ben and Kyle. He caught her eye and nodded before being drawn back into conversation.

CHAPTER 57

Later, as dessert and toasts wrapped up, Beth and Hope strolled around the tent arm in arm. Suddenly baby Ben ran by with a hunk of javelina cake in his fists, Ruthie hot on his trail. She hobbled grabbing tables and chairs as she pursued him, chocolate icing smeared on the bodice of her dress. Beth and Hope came to stand with Ben and Maggie, who were also watching the melee.

"Okay, that's enough," Maggie said, turning to her husband. "I know Ruthie loves him but that surely not helping her leg. Time for us to take the hellion in hand."

Ben laughed. "I'll go."

"Get a wet towel before you grab him!" Maggie called, shaking her head as she turned to Beth and Hope. "They better get caregivers with nerves of steel for the day care cottage or he'll be suspended on day one."

"He's adorable," Hope said, smiling at Maggie Morgan, one of the loveliest women she knew, inside and out. Tonight Maggie wore a midnight-blue dress with a plunging neckline and off-the-shoulder sleeves. Every inch of the dress flattered her full figure, her auburn hair falling loose around her shoulders. She had regained weight lost in the aftermath of a devastating miscarriage and she looked healthy and vibrant. A glamourous earth mother, she seemed to be able to do it all. Raise two children, manage the stables, and act as co-director of Emma's Dream, their summer camp for disabled children.

"Adorable, huh? Depends on who you talk to," Maggie said as they watched Ben scoop up his son, holding him at arm's length as he attempted to wipe the child's sticky hands. The effort was futile and soon his jacket and slacks were streaked with brown stains.

"See what I mean?" Maggie added. "Now my new dress will be covered if I dance with my husband!"

When the band began, Robbie was standing with Harley and Willow. "Now's your chance, buddy," Harley said, grinning at him. "You've been avoiding her all night."

"What are you talking about?" Robbie asked, knowing full well what Harley meant.

"She looks amazing tonight," Willow said. "You should definitely go for it."

Robbie scowled. *Great, now I'm getting dating advice from a fifteen-year-old!* "Thanks, guys, but isn't this your cue to hit the dance floor?"

Harley shook his head. "No can do. Not till Mr. and Mrs. Barnes start us off."

They watched as Jeb led Amy to the middle of the floor.

"Barnes cleans up pretty well, doesn't he?" Ben Morgan said, joining them, a wriggly toddler under one arm.

"What about Amy?" Willow said. "She looks awesome!" And she did in a simple crepe gown, off-white, strapless, its bodice hugging her slender frame. The skirt like a silk fan swished as she walked arm and arm with her husband. Her auburn hair was swept up off her long, slender neck, desert flowers woven in her hair.

"She's a looker, alright, which is more than I can say for you, buddy," Harley said, eying his friend. "What the hell happened?"

"Monster Baby."

"Want me to watch him so you can dance with Maggie?" Willow asked shyly.

"Thanks, Will, but my mom just called Carmela. She's comin' to get him. Hey, brother," he said, turning to Robbie. "What are you doin' over here when your gorgeous woman's over there?"

"I asked him the same thing," Harley said.

"And?"

"Can we please drop it, guys?" Robbie said as Carmela appeared at the door of the tent. "There's your savior, big brother. Want me to take my nephew over?"

"Thanks, but I've got this one. No need for another poor schmuck to get covered in cake."

Ben headed across the tent, Robbie at his side. Spark was dancing with Amy now and Jeb with his mom as others joined in. "It's now or never," Robbie said under his breath as he veered off and headed in Hope's direction. He was about ten feet away when Buck Foster flashed in front of him and bowed to her.

"M'lady, may I have this dance?"

Hope had spied Robbie headed her way, so she was startled at Buck's appearance. She hesitated momentarily, glimpsed Robbie's face over Foster's shoulder, but then said, "Of course," and offered her hand to him.

As they headed to the middle of the floor, Buck chuckled and Hope turned to study him. "You did that on purpose, didn't you?"

"Absolutely. Someone has to light a fire under Morgan's ass. A little competition oughta do the trick."

"You are a wicked man, Buck Foster."

"And proud of it. I'd say two or three dances should do it."

CHAPTER 58

Buck's prediction proved to be right on the mark. At the conclusion of the third dance, Robbie stalked up. "My turn, Foster. Hope, would you dance with me? Please?"

"Told you so," Buck whispered as she nodded and took Robbie's hand.

"I thought you'd never ask," she said as he took her in his arms.

"I'm surprised Foster let you go." The band played "When a Man Loves a Woman." *How perfect*, he thought, *now that I've probably lost her.*

"He's just being friendly. He lives with a woman."

"Then where the hell is she?"

"Would you dial it back just a little and calm down, please?"

"Sorry."

As he pulled her closer, Hope felt him trembling and her heart softened. "She and Spark don't get along."

"Who?"

"Buck's girlfriend."

"Can we not talk about Foster right now?" he asked.

"You started it."

"Okay, guilty as charged," he said, lips nuzzling her neck.

"What do you want to talk about?" she asked, shivering from neck to toes.

"Who says I want to talk?" he said, trailing kisses up and down her neck now.

"Don't start something you can't stop, Morgan."

Surprised at her brazen tone, he leaned back, studying her. "Who says I want to stop? You are the same woman I made love to two nights ago, aren't you?"

She smiled, her eyes mischievous. "The very same."

"Did something happen to you? Did you hit your head? Fall off your horse?"

"No, but time isn't on my side, is it? You're leaving on Monday, aren't you?" She drew close, pressing her body against his as they began swaying to the music. She could barely breathe. His erection tickled her belly, sending spasms of longing through her. *Oh, I will miss you, Robbie Morgan.*

The next dance, Bonnie Raitt's "Something to Talk About," was clearly a favorite of Jeb and Amy's, as they vamped their way around the dance floor. After watching the bride and groom for a minute or two, Robbie grabbed her, pulled her close, and began a swaying, rhythmic variation on the bump and grind. "Thank God for loose pants," he whispered as he led her around, Hope following his every move. He was a great dancer and they fit each other perfectly.

"Will you look at that?" Ben Senior said, pulling Leonora closer. "Looks like they've made up."

"Well, I wish they'd be a little more discreet," Leonora said. "We certainly did not teach our children to have sex on the dance floor!"

Her husband laughed, kissing the top of her head. "Now, Nora, we've gotten pretty close to that ourselves."

"Don't be ridiculous," she said, elbowing him even as she grinned.

"Watchin' the dirty dancing?" Kyle asked, coming to stand beside them.

"Don't be fresh!" Leonora said.

"They're not the only ones," Spark said, clapping his friend's back. "Look at my two! Is that any way for the bride and groom to be acting?"

"Well, this is the wild west," Kyle said. "I'm a little jealous. Where the hell are all the single women?"

"I know, baby," his mother said, patting his cheek. "Too bad Dara is out of town." She referred to Dara Littlefield, a friend of Maggie's he had dated a few times in the past.

"Okay, let's go, Nora," Spark said, grabbing hold of her. "You owe me a dance. Let's give the kids somethin' to talk about."

At that moment, Ruthie danced up and grabbed her dad. "Come on, handsome, let's go!"

The next song was Clapton's "Wonderful Tonight," one of Jeb's favorites. As he drew his bride close, the look of love in his eyes took Hope's breath away. She looked up and Robbie's eyes met hers, a longing so raw and open in his gaze. She reached up and stroked his chest, her other arm circling his neck. Before she knew it, his lips were on hers, locked in a deep, passionate kiss.

"Wonderful tonight" doesn't even come close, he thought as they swayed to the music. "You look beautiful, by the way."

"Thanks. You look pretty handsome yourself," she said, moving closer. *How will I ever say good-bye?*

As the dance ended, he whispered, "Wanta get out of here?"

"Won't that be rude?"

"Naw, everyone's watching the bride and groom."

As his brother and Hope walked hand in hand out the back door of the tent, Ben said to Maggie, "There goes trouble."

"Why? I thought they were crazy about each other."

"He's leaving tomorrow."

"I thought not till Monday?"

"Apparently, they called him back sooner. Goodbyes won't be pretty."

"You never know, nosey Parker. Now dance with me, my sweetheart. Then Emma wants the next one."

"You look glorious tonight, Mrs. Morgan. Think there'll be energy left after we get the rascals down?"

"There better be, Mr. Morgan, especially when you tease me with that," she said, gazing below his belt.

"I'm just happy I'm not wearing jeans," he said, drawing her closer as he swung her around the dance floor.

CHAPTER 59

They walked around the edge of the tent, Robbie's arm around her waist. "Wanta drive to the cabin?"

"No, we can't do that." She leaned over and kissed his neck as they skirted the massive barn.

"Wanta lay down on some of Spark's shiny new grass?"

"In this new dress? No way, cowboy, even for you."

"You got any ideas?"

"Let's keep walking and see if anyplace presents itself."

"You are a loose woman, aren't you?"

"Maybe," she said as they reached the south side of the enormous, rambling house and headed east.

As they passed the south-facing sun porch, she took both his hands. "Come here, cowboy."

"You think the porch is open?"

"Never mind the porch," she said, leaning against the smooth tile of a south-facing wall, still warm from the day's heat. "I'm happy right here."

His libido in overdrive, Robbie pressed his hands against wall above her shoulders, feeling the warmth as he kissed her deeply. "Works for me," he said huskily, one hand moving down to caress her breast, his mouth everywhere.

Hope moaned and tried to draw him closer, but he resisted, keeping her at arm's length as he kissed her and stroked her. He smiled as her breath grew shorter.

She sighed, "oh, oh, oh," afraid to cry out lest they be heard. As she climaxed, she opened her eyes and found him watching her, his eyes soft. "Pretty pleased with yourself, aren't you cowboy?" she said, aware of the wetness between her thighs as she reached over and began rubbing and stroking his erection.

"Pleased and not sure this cowboy can hang on much longer."

"Well, what are you waiting for?"

"Not a goddamn thing." He lifted her dress and slipped her panties off, spreading her legs. "Oh, darlin', you are so ready, aren't you?" he said as his fingers slipped between her thighs.

"You have no idea," she whispered, unzipping his fly and releasing him.

Robbie lifted her, wrapping her legs around his waist as he entered her, a tentative thrust, then a little more.

Before he could plunge deeper, she grabbed his buttocks and pulled him in.

"Please, please, please," she gasped. "I need you, all the way, now."

"No argument here, sweetheart," he said as he plunged full and deep, her back pressed against the wall. In seconds, he was lost in a tide of oblivion, every inch of him deep inside, as Hope embraced him all.

"Oh, I love you!," he cried.

Hope couldn't get enough of him, every fiber of her being on fire. "Oh, oh, oh, my love," she whispered. "Please don't stop! Never, never stop!"

As they reached thunderous, simultaneous orgasms, she heard voices and realized that people were walking nearby. Robbie's pants were at his ankles and her panties were goodness knew where. "Do you hear that?" she whispered, hair limp and damp on her neck.

"Sure do," he said, slipping out of her, shielding her from view as he pulled up his pants just as his brother and Maggie rounded the corner. Robbie slipped Hope's panties into his pocket.

As they came face to face with the others, Hope smoothed her skirt into place. Maggie jumped. "Oh!" she exclaimed.

Ben chuckled. "Well, well, hey, guys, guess we all had the same idea."

"Oh, my, we're so sorry," Maggie said, noticing the state of Hope's hair and dress, her brother-in-law's shirt untucked and rumpled.

Still weak from their lovemaking, Hope struggled to catch her breath. "No need to be sorry. It's us…it's just…we were," and then she burst out laughing.

"We get the 'we were' part," Ben said, also laughing. "This is sure to become part of family lore for generations to come."

"Not if I kill you first," Robbie said, all four of them laughing now.

"Leave it to Spark to plan a wedding under a full moon or we might've missed you," Maggie said.

"That guy thinks of everything," Robbie said drolly. "With his billions, he probably ordered the moon."

"Well, we'll leave you to it," Ben said. "Come on, Mags. We'll have to find our own spot." She giggled as they strolled off, disappearing around a jutting wing of the house.

"Oh, Lord," Hope said, pressing her head against Robbie's chest. "Do you think everyone will know by the time we get back?"

"Not if they find a place of their own," he said, lifting her chin, kissing her softly. "You are amazing, sweetheart. Just when I think I know you, you surprise me, big-time."

Not daring to meet his eyes, she said, "I'll miss you."

"We have talk about that."

No, no, no, don't spoil the moment talking about our nonexistent future. "We better get back," she said, grabbing her shawl from the ground. She took his hand and began walking quickly now, toward the enormous tent that glowed like a rosy world of warmth at the edge of Spark Foster's extraordinary home.

When they reached the edge of the tent, they found Beth and Lang at the doorway. "Oh, Hope, hi," she said, waving. "We've gotta go and relieve Martha and Neecy."

"Wait, I'll go with you," Hope said. "Just have to grab my purse." She let go of Robbie's hand and hurried to their table, grabbing her small clutch. He followed, catching her as she started back toward the door of the tent.

He grasped her arm. "Hey, I can take you home."

"It's better this way," she said, slipping out of his grasp.

"I was going to suggest a night at the cabin." His kind eyes pleaded with her, sadness dancing around them.

"I can't, Robbie. I'm sorry."

"You're coming to breakfast, aren't you?"

"Of course. I'll see you then." She leaned forward, kissing his cheek as she practically sprinted out the door.

"Out of reach again," a voice said to his right.

Robbie turned to spy Buck Foster. "It's none of your business, Foster."

"Extraordinary woman like that is everyone's business. Don't be stupid, Morgan."

The man is right, of course, and I'm a fool. I'll make it up to her in the morning. He stalked off without a word, headed for the bar, leaving Foster grinning like the Cheshire Cat.

CHAPTER 60

Hope woke to a warm, sunny day. Every inch of her body ached after a restless night full of dreams and terrors. *Too much wine,* she decided, pulling on her jeans. During one of her wakeful ruminations, she hadmade a decision. She would not go to the breakfast. *Better to have last night and not go through the agony of saying good-bye.*

She found Beth and Lang in the kitchen, fruit and coffee on the table. "Hey, sleepyhead. Wanta join us?" she asked.

"No thanks. I feel awful. I think I'm coming down with something." She held her belly, doing her best imitation of an invalid with a stomachache.

Beth saw right through her. "Oh, no you don't! You're coming with us. They'll be a million people. Besides, don't you want to say good-bye?"

"That's my cue," Lang said, rising. "I'll go get Miss Lil changed." He scooped up the baby and disappeared.

"We said good-bye last night."

"Not from my observation."

"Please, Beth, it's over. This is for the best."

"For who?"

"For your brother." Stomach problems forgotten, she poured a mug of coffee and stirred spoonfuls of sugar and cream into it.

"I doubt he'd agree. Have you talked to him about it?"

"If you're referring to my barren womb, I told you, yes, we talked about it."

"I mean again, after the first time?"

"No."

"Then you should."

"It's no good. I can't give him what he deserves."

"Not the houseful of Morgan clones again?"

"You wouldn't understand. You've grown up in this beautiful, loving bubble. The rest of us haven't been so lucky."

"Hope, this is craziness. Please come with us."

"I'm sorry. I can't. Please tell everyone I'm sick."

She sat on the front porch, waving as Lang, Beth, and Lily drove off, then realized that the moment Robbie saw them, he'd come after her. She went in, pulled on her boots, grabbed her keys, and headed to the truck. *A long ride'll do me good.*

She expected the stables to be empty, so was surprised to spy Nick Parker's old, battered truck. She walked through the barn, the horses nickering softly as she passed by. The intoxicating scent of fresh straw was calming, and she took a deep breath.

"Hey, good morning," he called from Rowdy's stall, startling her out of her reverie. His handsome face was already smeared with dirt, bits of straw all over him.

"Oh, Nick, good morning. Why aren't you up at the house?"

"Not family."

"But surely you were invited?"

"Not my scene, you know? I mean, the Morgans are great. Don't get me wrong, but I like the quiet of the barn, and someone needed to be down here this morning. I'll go over to the Fosters' later to say good-bye to the newlyweds."

"I thought they left last night?"

"Nope, they were at a B and B in town. They fly to Hawaii tonight."

"Lucky them. Nick, I'd like to take Whimsy out."

"No problem. I'll saddle her."

"No, you keep at it in there. I can do it."

"Suit yourself. All her stuff is in the tack room."

It was a cool morning, perfect for a long ride. She had been out often enough that she knew the trails and decided to head northwest along the curving Barrel Ridge. As she led Whimsy out of the barn, Nick called, "Wait up!"

He popped his head out of the stall and said, "Where you headed?"

"Does it matter?"

"Ranch rules. We need to know your flight plan."

She smiled. "I thought I'd follow the Barrel Ridge, then head back, skirting the open meadows just east of the farm."

"Okay, but be careful on the Barrel. I doubt that horse has been out there in a while, if ever. Take it slow."

"Will do," she said, waving as she headed off.

CHAPTER 61

Robbie spied his sister and Lang come in, late as usual. Everyone was seated and Leonora had insisted they begin eating while the food was hot. He hopped up from the table and caught Beth in the hallway. "Where is she?"

His father and mother exchanged glances as they came to greet them. "Hey, you two, better late than never," Ben Senior said, kissing his daughter. "Where's your nanny?"

"Sick. She stayed in bed. Thinks she's coming down with something."

"Well, that won't be good for the baby. She'd better move over here until she's fully recuperated."

"Come on, darlin', let 'em eat. Everyone, come on in."

Robbie sat back down, ate a few bites, then jumped up. Without a word, he disappeared through the kitchen door.

His mother frowned. "Robert, where are you going?"

"Let him be, Nora."

"But it's his last morning!"

"He'll be back. Now, everyone, eat," he said, ruffling Emma's curls. Her place was always between her beloved grandfathers, Ben Morgan at the head of the table on one side, Ned Williams, Maggie's dad, on her other side.

CHAPTER 62

Robbie jumped in the truck and tore out of the driveway. When he reached the house, he called out, his voice echoing in the empty house. Undaunted, he took the stairs two at a time, not surprised to find Hope's room and bed empty since her truck was not in the driveway. Suspecting where she would be, he headed downstairs and into Lang's study. He opened the desk drawer where his brother-in-law kept his cigars, smoked only on rare occasions by the family health nut. Robbie grabbed a cigar and slipped off its paper ring, gently tucking it into his pocket.

He pulled up to the barn, spying Hope's truck. Nick Parker was in the east corral, walking one of the Friesians. "Where is she?"

"Out."

"Which way did she go?"

Nick hesitated, unsure what he should do.

"Parker, if you don't tell me this instant, I'll have you fired."

"Yeah, right. She's following the Barrel, but I'm pretty sure she wants to be alone."

"Jesus Christ," he said, running into the barn and grabbing Rowdy's tack.

The strong stallion galloped to the base of the Ridge trail, then slowed as they began the ascent. Hope was nowhere to be seen, but he pressed on until they reached the top of the ridge. In the far distance he could see them beginning their descent back to the valley floor. Rowdy paused, unsure of his footing, and for a second Robbie considered turning back. His oldest brother would kill him if anything happened to his horse.

Slowly he urged the sorrel quarter horse forward, and Rowdy found his footing. As they reached the trailhead leading downward, he could see Hope a mile ahead. She and Whimsy were midway across the meadow. Allowing Rowdy to feel his way, they descended cautiously, Robbie keeping Hope in sight. When they reached level ground, he called, "Hah," and heeled Rowdy's flank. The horse took off at a gallop, closing the distance between them as Robbie held on tight.

As they neared, Hope turned, startled at the sight of horse and rider bearing down on them. "Whoa, girl," she said, steadying her horse, waiting.

"Robbie, what in the world?" she cried as he slowed to a trot and jumped from his horse.

"Please, Hope, I need to talk to you." He held out his hands, which she ignored, turning away to dismount herself.

"This is crazy. What are you doing?"

"This," he said, coming to stand in front of her. As he caught his breath, he began fishing around inside his jacket. When he found what he sought, he palmed it and knelt down. "Hope Seymour, I love you more than anything in the world. I know I cannot live another day knowing that you will not in my life. I don't care where we live. I don't care about the baby thing. I don't care about anything as long as you're with me. Please put me out of my misery and say you'll marry me."

A tear trickled down her cheek. "But you love children. I know you do!"

"Yes, I do, but what does that have to do with anything?"

"It has everything to do with it. I can't give you that."

"Of course you can, sweetheart. We can adopt. Look at Toby. Jeb and Amy couldn't love him any more if he were their own flesh and blood. You'll make an incredible mother, and I'd like to think I'll do okay as a dad. Please say yes."

Hope wiped her tears and looked down at him. "Well, if you don't have the good sense to run back to Sedona, I guess I'll have to marry you. I'm sure it's obvious that I've been in love with you since day one. Now please get up and give me a kiss, cowboy."

"Wait, there's more," he said, taking her left hand in his and slipping the paper cigar ring onto her finger. "This is only temporary until we can shop for one you like."

"Oh, Robbie, I love you so much," she said, falling into his arms, their bodies a tangle in the tall meadow grass.

"Sweetheart, while I'd love to tear your clothes off and make wild passionate love to you, I'm scared to death of ticks and rattlesnakes. How about we make a date for tonight at the cabin?"

Eyes shining with happiness, she kissed him. "Are you sure about the snakes and ticks thing?"

"Just as sure as I am that I love you beyond all reason, Hope Seymour. Shall we ride back on flat ground and tell the others?"

"First give me one more kiss," she said, standing and wrapping her arms around his neck.

"My pleasure," he said as the horses nickered softly around them, the tall grass swishing in the breeze.

EPILOGUE

After telling the family their news, Robbie and Hope headed to the cabin for a few hours. Lang and Sam Morgan took a late afternoon jog and spied their trucks parked side by side at the base of the cabin road. "Wanta guess what they're doing?" Lang asked.

Sam laughed. "My brother and your nanny. What's the world coming to?"

"Pretty scandalous. Why didn't we know about this love nest when Beth and I were dating?" Lang asked.

"For this very reason," Sam said, pointing to the cars. "Beth would never have wanted anyone to see her truck or your Rover parked in plain view for all the world to see. There's only one reason people go up there and it's not to bird-watch. I never brought Rose here, either. Wasn't ready for the ranch hotline to kick into high gear."

"True."

"So, are you out a nanny?"

"Not for a while. Hope assures me she's staying as long as we need her. Truth be told, I'd love it if Beth would take a year or two off, even longer, but I think it would drive her crazy. Between Hope, your mom, my mom, Neecy, and Carmela, we'll hang on till your parents get the cottage up and running."

"Gonna be cool," Sam said. "And not just cause I worked on the plans."

As the two men turned on to the Loop Trail, Sam said, "Should we have stopped in to say hello?"

"Not if we want to remain among the living."

Their laughter echoed on the dusty trail.

*****

Hope and Robbie lay in each other's arms after making love. It was not the first time, but this last was languid and loving, each gazing into the other's eyes, souls and spirits joined in a space beyond words. Bodies slick with sweat, they lay spent and sated. Hope kissed his shoulder, her fingers running through his hair. "I love you," she whispered, nibbling his earlobe.

"Me, too, you," he said. "But the truth is I couldn't possibly put into words how I feel, my beloved fiancée. I never thought I'd feel this way about a woman. Ever."

"And I never thought I'd feel this way about a man," she said. "You've awakened and roused parts of me that I didn't even know I had, Robbie Morgan."

"Good," he said. "And speaking of roused, I can't believe it, but you've done it again."

"Mmm…I feel that," she said, swiveling her hips, squeezing and caressing him deeply. "Oh, God, does that feel amazing, you growing inside me."

"Come to me, darlin'," he said, wrapping her legs around him as he plunged into her luscious, hidden depths. Their rhythmic dance began again.

*****

"Hey, sleepyhead," he whispered, realizing that they had been asleep for several hours.

She opened her eyes and smiled, drunk with lovemaking. "What time is it?"

"About five. I've gotta get on the road."

"I thought you were leaving Monday? Do you have to go?" she asked, drawing him closer.

"'Fraid so, but I'll be back soon."

"Not sure I'll even be here. I might be fired as the worst nanny in the world."

"I thought Sunday was your day off?"

"It is, but I still feel guilty."

"Well, don't. Lang and Beth have lots of help."

"What will your coworkers say about your news?"

"They'll think it's great."

"Even Jane?"

"Had to slip that in, didn't you?"

She tickled him. "Sorry!"

"Cut that out, you vixen. They will *all* be happy for us, but not about the rest of my news."

"Oh?"

"I'm quitting. I'll stay on till they find a new person to work with Dave, unless they give me the boot out of spite."

"What will you do?"

"I've been talkin' to Dad. There are a couple of possibilities, although running adventure tours here isn't one of them. Don't want to spoil the valley. We can talk later. I really don't care where I am as long as it's with you. We can live around here, or down your way."

"You'd do that?"

"Well, I just assumed you'd want to keep your shop and your connections in Tintown?"

"I love you, Robbie Morgan."

"I know," he said, kissing the tip of her nose. "And we'll figure out logistics as we go along."

"Yes, we will."

Please read on for chapters from **Widow's Island!**

Widow's Island

Biologist Ned Fielding leaves the tattered remains of his marriage behind to spend six months on Winward Island, a property shared by SENCA, his land conservation group, and the reclusive Widow Barlow. Dispatched to the island to study a rare species of carrion beetle, Ned finds himself much more interested in studying the island's only other human, the beautiful Addie Barlow, whose screams of terror awaken him in the dead of night.

A hurricane and near drowning throw the island's two inhabitants together, and they begin a smoldering love affair. The locals call the Widow Barlow a witch and enchantress. They claim she murdered her much older husband, the philanthropist King Barlow, but Ned cannot quite believe the wild tales about the gentle woman he adores. Enchantress, maybe—with her closest companions an osprey, a dolphin, and a coyote— but murderess? Will Ned's quest for the truth destroy their love and Addie's heart?

SAMPLE CHAPTERS OF WIDOW'S ISLAND CHAPTER 1

"You can't send that nitwit Peterson to do the job. Jesus, Marty! The last census we sent him out on was so fucked up it had to be completely redone."

"Then who do you suggest, Phil? Margot's on Block Island till August and Ray's wife'd never cut him loose for that long; six months is a long time to be away from the family. That's why Andy'd be so perfect. No wife, no kids, practically no friends, and…"

"Forget it. I'll call Ned. He's the best person for the job, anyway."

"Fielding? You gotta be kidding! Penny'd never let him out of his cage for six months!"

"Penny's got nothin' to do with it—they're separated."

"Too bad…I didn't know. Not that it's a surprise; mismatched couple of the century, if you ask me. Mrs. Society and Mr. Limpet. Geez, how'd they ever hook up in the first place?"

"Married when they were kids; baby already on the way. Some people grow up together in those kinda marriages. Some don't. Anyway, Ned'd be glad of the chance to get away, I'll bet. It's been pretty nasty on the home front from what he tells me."

"Still under the same roof?"

"He's lookin', but they're still sharing the house. She's away right now, I think, with orders for him to be gone before she gets back. His family's house, too. 'Bout the only thing he brought to the marriage and Penny wants it. Sickening when you think of all the Pardington millions she has to throw around."

"Good old Ned. Penny's always been a bitch."

"Marty, I haven't got time for this right now," the older man interrupted, feeling like a traitor for gossiping about his friend's marriage. "I'll call Ned and if he can't go, better start packing. Someone's gotta be on the Winward Island by the middle of the month. *Nicrophorus americanus*, if they're there, will be emerging by then, and we want a complete study covering the whole six months till dormancy."

"I'll be in Portsmouth if you need me. Later, Phil."

Marty Robinson left his friend to sort through the disheveled mess on his desk. Phil couldn't remember Ned Fielding's phone number, didn't keep a rolodex or an address book, and his blotter, where the number was jotted down, was buried under a mountain of papers. Shifting the pile back and forth several times, he peeked cautiously underneath each corner. As he moved toward the middle of the blotter, he started a landslide of bills, flyers, and grant proposals. The pile picked up steam, scooping up an overburdened vertical file in a downward rush. "Shit!" he muttered, watching the last of the papers cascade over the floor, some coming to rest under the water cooler, others floating into an open aquarium. "Sorry, Boris," he said, lunging to remove a stack of Chace Point Bird Sanctuary brochures from the back of a baby snapping turtle, too startled by the sudden onslaught to snap at him.

Turning back to the desk, he spied Fielding's number scribbled on the now-emptied blotter. He dialed. Busy. Leaning back, he closed his eyes for several minutes. It had been a hard year for SENCA, the Southeastern Natural Conservation Agency, of which he was president. The whole region was in a recession, and state and federal funding had been slashed. The first thing to go had been Phil's secretary, Edna, who had been with him since the beginning—almost twenty years. They'd been good years, he reflected. He missed Edna. Actually, she'd been ready to retire. He could easily hire part-time help, but he figured he'd save money, and besides, he hated to break in a new person and have her poking around in his and Edna's stuff.

And SENCA was in better shape than most. They had a generous endowment—lots of folks remembered them in their wills and the money had been invested prudently. King Barlow's gift alone would keep them in operation for twenty or thirty years. And in addition to the money, he had bequeathed Winward Island—half of it, anyway—to the agency in his will. The island had been the one holding they had neglected, until now.

On an unauthorized day trip, a couple of college kids, SENCA volunteers, had discovered what they believed to be Giant Carrion beetles, *Nicrophorus americanus*, on the island. A rare species of burying beetles, *Nicrophorus americanus* had been thought to be extinct until their discovery in recent years on Block Island. Now they might also be present on Winward. The importance of this study dictated that he must send a decent researcher. Ned Fielding was overqualified for this type of field study, but the only man within the agency whom Phil trusted to do the job right.

They hadn't sent anyone to the island since its acquisition twelve years earlier. It was time to conduct a complete census of the plant and animal life, time to map it out and give the island the attention it deserved. Its location along the Atlantic Flyway alone made it an important, extremely valuable acquisition.

He tried Fielding again. This time the phone rang four times before Ned picked it up.

"Ned, hey, it's Phil."

"Hi, Phil!"

"How are things going?"

"'Bout the same. You know about Penny and me. There's not much more to say."

"It's been great having your help at Chace Point this spring. Wish we could pay you more, but…"

"Hey, I've enjoyed myself. Ray and I just got the nest platform up on the spit—East Marsh—and we're lookin' for a new project."

"That's the reason I'm calling. You got a place to live yet, buddy?"

"I think I've got a place out near Watuppa Pond—friend of a friend. Gonna rent for a while, till I get things straightened out. Why?"

"Well, if you're free to get away for a while, I have a job for you. Winward Island. Ever heard of it?"

"Yeah, off the coast near Derryville. Barrier Island—we own it, don't we? SENCA, I mean."

"Yup—it's one of our few undiscovered frontiers. We need a complete census, soil samples, beach study, and surveying. Giant Carrion beetles have been found out there, you know."

"No, I didn't. Wow! After Block Island, that should be…"

"Let me qualify my statement. Grad students may have found the beetles last summer. They took some pretty amazing photos. No samples, though. Just pictures. Only there a few hours. Typical. But listen, buddy, if the beetles are there, we could work with the Block Island people on a recovery plan to bring them back. We need you for that, Ned. What do you say—you game?"

"Sounds good. How much time you talking about?"

"At least six months, maybe more."

"Phil, I'd love to, but…with the divorce and all, I'm not sure I could get away for that long. Can I get back to you later?"

"Sure. I can give you a couple of days, but don't wait too long, buddy. Someone's gotta be out there by the middle of the month, and I'll have to get Peterson or Ray if you can't."

"I'll let you know tomorrow. Thanks, Phil."

CHAPTER 2

Ned debated an hour or two before calling Penny at the beach house to which she had retreated—until he "vacated her home." She reacted with typical venom, but Ned, stoic and unmoved, ignored her. They had been living apart emotionally for so many years, a few extra months wouldn't hurt before their ties were legally severed. He just didn't care anymore. Didn't care if she took the house, the antiques, the dog—although he'd miss Haggardy. Penny didn't even like Haggardy. She was keeping him for spite.

"I can't believe how selfish you are, Ned. But then you've always put yourself first, before me, before the kids, before your social obligations, before everything. For God's sakes, couldn't you think of me just this once? How am I going to get on with my life if you leave me dangling here for six months while you're off counting bugs?"

"Do you want to get remarried right away, Penny?"

"Are you kidding? After what you put me through, I'll never marry again!"

"Then what does it matter, really? Six months isn't long after all the years we've…"

"Don't even say it, Ned! I will not have our estrangement become public knowledge. In fact, I'm having Martin draw up gag orders to that effect. I will not have my reputation ruined by gossip, and I'll thank you to speak to no one about our affairs, past or present, until the papers are drawn up."

"Penny, relax. Everyone knows. It's not exactly a surprise. Can we just let it go for now? I'm going to Winward and I'll be back the end of October, beginning of November. We can sign papers then, or if you can't wait, I can come back for a day to take care of things whenever you and Martin have documents ready."

"What about the settlement? What about all the details, the division of property, the…"

"You handle it, Pen. Whatever you think is fair. Have it all if you want. I…"

"Isn't that typical! Once again, I have to do it all. Isn't there anything you want?"

"My clothes, tools, and…"

"Yes…here it comes. I knew it."

"Well, if you'd like, I could take Haggardy. He's a…"

"Forget it! Just forget it, Ned! I wouldn't dream of sending Haggardy to some godforsaken island, probably loaded with deer ticks and fleas! Besides, he belongs to me."

"Fine, Pen. Listen—I gotta go. I'll send you an address where I can be reached and I'll call the kids, too."

"That's the other thing, the children. Are they supposed to wait six months, too, to have this settled, to see you, to…?"

"I'll call them, Penny. If they have strong objections, I won't go, okay? Now, I've really got to go."

"Fine, I'm late for an appointment! You'll be hearing from Martin soon. Good-bye."

She clicked the phone down before he could say good-bye, anything to get the last word.

He put off calling the kids until the evening, but he called Phil and accepted the job. Neither Ned Jr. nor Sydney, his daughter, would care, he knew, but he'd check with them anyway.

CHAPTER 3

Icy pearls of sunlit water fell noiselessly from the paddles as the kayak glided through the channel rounding the east end of Winward Island. With spring, Addie spent her mornings, just after sunrise, paddling in the marshes. A net and several empty burlap bags lay ready, stuffed in the prow beside her feet, should they be needed. But pleasure, not work, drove her to the sea in the early morning hours.

The day was clear and crisp. The April morning air embraced her with cloying chilliness. The marsh beckoned, reaching out to envelop her in its magical green depths, but thoughts intruded, distracting her from the rustling beauty that surrounded her. Usually she paddled hard for a time, then lifted the paddles and drifted, listening to the sea birds screeching and calling, the fish jumping, and the rustle of the spartina…soft and soothing, but today she paddled ferociously as if driven by unseen demons, faster and faster until beads of sweat dotted her brow and her arms burned with the strain of exertion.

Her home was about to be invaded and there was absolutely nothing she could do about it. For twelve years, she had lived alone on the island. Now her sanctuary, her peaceful world was to be taken over, perhaps forever. Who would they send? Would there be more than one? Would they disregard the boundaries and trespass onto her side of the island?

The trustees of her husband's estate had assured her the conservation agency that shared the island with her would respect her privacy. They owned thirty acres, she twenty. The island was to be kept as a wildlife sanctuary. No building, no camping, no human habitation was planned for Winward Island, the name they had given it upon taking possession. Now they were sending someone to live for six months on her island. Six months!

She knew she was lucky to have the land at all. So many times over those last precarious months, King had threatened to take it away, threatened to will the entire island to SENCA and let them have her cottage, her gardens, everything. He'd laughed and taunted her continuously, knowing that Winward was her only refuge, her only love. She didn't love him, had never loved him. But King Barlow had died suddenly, before he could change his will, and his widow had inherited the cottage and its surrounding acreage, the fields, ponds, gardens, and thicket. She also owned the cove with its many caves hidden beneath the cliffs, where she loved to explore.

The dock was in the cove, the only easy access to the island, hence the reason SENCA had contacted her in the first place, to request permission to use her dock. Recognizing the futility of refusing, she had written back giving her consent and requested that they use the west footpath to reach their property, rather than the more direct path running north to south that traversed her fields. The reply assured her that the agency would respect her privacy, keeping to the western footpath when venturing forth from the dock. "Rest easy, Mrs. Barlow," the letter had ended. "Our people will try not to pester you in the slightest way. We are as eager as you are to ensure that Winward remains undisturbed and peaceful. Please contact me personally if there is any problem whatsoever. Phillip K. Bodington, Director, SENCA."

The letter from Mr. Bodington had not reassured her, especially the part about "our people." Was there to be a whole bevy of scientists crawling over the island for six months? Would there also be a steady stream of visitors taking part in the study? Visions of boatloads of college students descending upon Winward made her shudder, and the paddle jabbed unevenly beneath the glassy surface of the water, the handle nearly jerking free of her grasp.

Glimpsing a crab, its broad swimming legs catching the sunlight as he paddled sideways through the eel grass, she swung the net, a flawless extension of her right arm, and scooped him up, wetting the burlap bag with her left hand as she tossed him in. The action, completed in a few seconds' time, appeared to be almost reflexive, after which she continued paddling, worries consuming her still.

After an hour's time, she headed back, a bag full of crabs, heart and mind no lighter, but resigned. Dropping the crabs in one of the pots near shore, she paddled in and pulled the kayak up onto the beach. She kept her fishing scow tied to the dock, but she preferred to drag the lighter craft up onto the beach. That way it could be more easily carried to higher ground if a storm threatened, or she could drag it over the ridge for use in the pond near the cottage. She scanned the surface of the water closely for some minutes before turning to head up the path lined with rose hips and honeysuckle that led back to the cottage.

As she entered the thicket, she heard a familiar screech. She turned in time to spy a huge bird dropping from the vast blue above her, its talons outstretched as it fell. Pulling a leather glove from her pocket, she slipped it onto her right hand, stretching her arm out straight to her side. Sharp talons dug into the leather as the osprey came to rest, grasping her gloved hand. "Gwydyon, son of Don." She smiled, stroking his feathers. "How goes it with you this fine day?"

The fish hawk bowed his head, enjoying the attention, alternately gazing from his mistress to the sea. "I have nothing for you this morning. Maybe later." As she talked, she walked slowly along the path through the thicket. When it became clear that no meal was forthcoming, Gwydyon became restless. "Just a minute, my friend," she cooed, quickening her pace.

He was vulnerable to attack in the thicket, so she hated to release him lest his flight be checked by an unforeseen enemy. Without food, he was probably safe, but there were several golden eagles and great horned owls that frequented the island. While they rarely challenged Gwydyon on the open water, where he was pestered instead by terns continually lying in wait to steal his catch, they might hazard a skirmish in the brush, where his sharp, lashing talons were less effective.

Finally she reached the open fields. From there, the path ran straight through the meadows to the shingled cottage just visible in the distance. The bird arched his wings, rearing back. Addie released him with an upward thrust and his powerful wings carried him aloft. As soon as he reached a safe height, he circled once, screeching farewell as he disappeared over the treetops toward the open sea.

Walking on, she stared ahead at the whitewashed cottage, her home for the past twelve years. Built seventeen years earlier, at the time of her marriage, the cottage had been winterized when Addie had settled permanently on the island. It had two stories, with a wide porch wrapped around its front and sides. The faded, white-shingled walls were alive with climbing greenery. English ivy crept high under the second-story windows and intertwined with clematis vines, the blue and white flowers not yet in bloom. The vegetation at first gave the impression of wild abandon, belying the hours of cultivation and care that made their existence possible.

A two-story barn with a lean-to shed and greenhouse attached stood behind the house to the south. The land gently sloped from the back of the cottage so that the taller, more imposing barn faded gracefully into the receding landscape rather than overwhelming the much smaller house. Its brown, weathered sides blended comfortably with the woods to the east, at harmony with its surroundings.

As she approached the cottage, a yelp of greeting hailed her as a tawny beast bounded up, flinging her front paws around her mistress. Laughing, Addie knelt beside her pet, ruffling the soft fur on the animal's back. "Aran! So you finally decided to wake up! No swim for you this morning!"

Woman and beast went together into the cottage, where she fed her pet, fixing tea for herself. Sipping it slowly, she sat at the worn table fashioned with her own hands from wood carted back from the mainland by boat. There was a salvage yard in Derryville she visited when she needed materials for the house, and she kept an old pickup truck on the mainland to use for these infrequent sojourns and for her deliveries of produce and fish. She hated driving, but as her client list had grown, the truck had become indispensable. The drop-off places along the river reached roughly half of her customers; the rest had to be delivered by truck.

During the spring, her days were freer; the garden was not yet in full flower and the fishing still sparse. The Massachusetts climate demanded caution in planting fragile, warm-weather crops, but her tomatoes, peppers, eggplants, and flowers were flourishing in the warm moisture of the greenhouse. She tended to them first, passing among the rows to give water and pinch back unwanted growth. The greenhouse, too, had been built entirely from salvage materials. Unlike the cottage and barn that her former husband had had built—as a wedding gifts to her—the greenhouse and shed had been constructed later on, after she had come to live on the island.

The first years she had survived on the small inheritance King had left her, tending a tiny garden for her own needs. When she began fishing, clamming, and lobstering to earn money, she expanded the garden, too. Once she began marketing her produce, she needed a hothouse. Rather than hiring someone to build it, she had undertaken the project herself. It had saved money, but more importantly, it had given her confidence and a feeling of self-sufficiency. Previously she had called upon plumbers, carpenters, electricians, and mechanics when things broke and needed repair, but since the completion of the shed and greenhouse ten years earlier, not another soul had set foot on the island. Whatever expertise she required came from books and her own experimentation.

Midday found her weeding and picking early spinach. She had already harvested parsnips and winter carrots, and her broccoli, cauliflower, and lettuces were well underway. She protected the lettuces at night and when the days were particularly cold, but the thick layer of mulch and the protected enclosure of the garden kept the plants relatively safe from a killing frost.

Until June she sold little of her produce, as most of her clients were seasonal residents who came to spend the summer at the beach. She had a few year-round customers who paid to have anything from her garden yield, as well as a share of her catch. What little money she made before June, however, came from the fish she sold to wholesalers. From June to October she sold only to her regular customers, unless there was a surplus. When summer cottages on the mainland coast were boarded up, she slowed down and moved into her winter schedule.

As the years went by, her customer list grew until she finally had to turn people away. She kept a waiting list of would-be customers only too eager to receive some of her weekly bounty, some offering double or triple the usual charge to be put "on the route." Addie refused to grow bigger, however, since the thought of having to hire help was abhorrent to her.

Each customer received three deliveries a week of fish, vegetables, herbs, flowers, and fruit. They paid a flat weekly fee, the same no matter what they received. When a new customer was taken on, they filled out a form with likes and dislikes. At that time, they selected which plan they desired: only fruit and vegetables; all five items—fish, vegetables, fruit, herbs and flowers; or just fish and flowers. While she attempted to cater to individual tastes, Addie brought a variety of offerings depending on what was ripe or what she'd managed to catch or dig or net on any given day. No one had ever complained, and the woven baskets brimming with fresh food were always a delightful surprise.

When the Widow's baskets arrived, dinner was planned around the bounty within them, whether it was steamers and corn, wild raspberries, apples, and blue crabs, or lobsters, arugula, and fresh scallions. Always there were flowers from early spring on—first tulips and daffodils, then iris, lupine, and wild sweet peas, then the zinnias, asters, cosmos, marigolds, coreopsis, snapdragons, dahlias, cornflowers, and all manner of wild flowers growing in riotous profusion in Winward's meadows.

This morning would be spent repairing her lobster traps in preparation for the following week, when they would be baited and set out for the first time. She also needed to make several new baskets as she had reluctantly agreed to take on four new clients this year. Some of the old baskets were worn and split, in need of repair. Fashioned from rushes, dried in the sunroom over the winter, the baskets were strong and water-resistant, their large willow handles smooth and comfortable to hold, even when they were heavily laden with produce. Along with the baskets, she sometimes used burlap sacks for her deliveries if she was bringing large quantities of shellfish.

Each customer was allotted two baskets and several bags per season, the empty ones to be returned with the following delivery. If a basket was lost or misplaced, she had begun charging for new ones. Some people feigned loss in order to have one of the simple but beautiful baskets to take home at the end of the season, so she was careful to set aside enough of the cattails and rushes for drying in order to replace worn or "misplaced" baskets. Several times customers had suggested that she might like to sell some baskets to the local gift shops or stores in the city, where, they assured her, she would make a handsome profit. Addie always declined.

As she went about her afternoon chores, she began to relax. They would stay on their side and she would stay far away. She knew every inch of the island and every hiding place. *Six months and they would be gone. She would find a way to bear it.*

About the Author

M. Lee Prescott is the author of dozens of works of fiction for adults, young adults, and children, among them **Prepped to Kill, Gadfly, Lost in Spindle City (Ricky Steele Mysteries), A Friend of Silence, In the Name of Silence and The Silence of Memory (Roger and Bess Mysteries), Jigsaw,** and **Song of the Spirit**, and her newest contemporary romance series, **Morgan's Run,** of which **Hope's Wonder** is the fifth! Three of her nonfiction titles have been published by Heinemann, and she has published numerous articles in the field of literacy education. Lee is a professor of education at a small New England liberal arts college, where she teaches reading and writing pedagogy. Her current research focuses on mindfulness and connections to reading and writing. She regularly teaches abroad, most recently in Singapore.

Lee has lived in southern California (loved those Laguna nights!), Chapel Hill, North Carolina, and various spots in Massachusetts and Rhode Island. Currently she resides in Massachusetts on a beautiful river, where she canoes, swims, and watches an incredible variety of wildlife pass by. She is the mother of two grown sons and spends lots of time with them, their beautiful wives, and her amazing grandchildren. When not teaching or writing, Lee's passions revolve around family, yoga (Kripalu is a second home), swimming, sharing mindfulness with children and adults, and walking.

Lee loves to hear from readers. Email her at mleeprescott@gmail.com, and visit her website to hear the latest and sign up for her newsletters!

AUTHOR WEBPAGE AND NEWSLETTER SIGN-UP HERE:

http://www.mleeprescott.com

A Note From the Author

I am thrilled to bring you Hope and Robbie's story, the fifth of the **Morgan's Run** series, with more coming soon! Thank you so much for reading it. These beloved characters will be around as the series continues to grow. The Morgan's Run books are set in the gorgeous American Southwest, an area of the country that is dear to my heart because it is home to my youngest son and family, but also because its beauty is so extraordinary and so startlingly different from that of my New England home. What a backdrop for romance and adventure!

If you like **Hope's Wonder** and would be willing to write an Amazon review, I would be very grateful. If you would like to sign up for future book releases and occasional notices about my books, please visit my Author Website: http://www. mleeprescott.com and sign up for my newsletter. I promise I will not share your address, nor will I flood you with emails. Do visit my site to read more about my books and hear what's next.

Finally, this book has been revised, proofed, and edited many, many times, but my intrepid assistants and I are human, so if you spot a typo, please email me at mleeprescott@gmail.com and I will fix it. If you'd like to know more about my other books, please scroll ahead to the next section, which is followed by sample chapters of **Widow's Island**, a sexy, stand-alone romance in my **Well-Loved** series.

Warm wishes,

M. Lee

Contemporary romances and mysteries by M. Lee Prescott include:

The Ricky Steele Mysteries

Book 1: Prepped to Kill

Book 2: Gadfly

Book 3: Lost in Spindle City

Also featuring Ricky Steele:

Jigsaw

Roger and Bess Mysteries

Book 1: A Friend of Silence

Book 2: In the Name of Silence

Book 3: The Silence of Memory

Contemporary Romances

Well-Loved Romances

Widow's Island

Hestor's Way

Morgan's Run Romances

Book 1: Emma's Dream

Book 2: Lang's Return

Book 3: Jeb's Promise

Book 4: Rose's Choice

Book 5: Hope's Wonder

Young Adult Historical Romance

Song of the Spirit